Beneath
Freedom's Wing

Caroline Grimm

Caroline D. Grimm

DEDICATION

For Heidi Caton

A true friend who knows my skeletons on a first name basis.

And for all those who continue to fight for true equality…

beneath freedom's wing.

ACKNOWLEDGMENTS

A wonderful year has passed since the publication of Wild Sweeps the Wind, Book One of the Voices of Pondicherry series. It amazes me the number of new friends who entered my life because they embraced Phebe Beach's story. Although I helped bring the book to life, it was Phebe's book all along. She gave it the spirit and the humor and the pathos. The girl wanted her story told, and I was glad to be of some service in her plan.

And now here you are, dear reader, about to embark on another journey with me. Within these pages you will find the story of our Phebe's aunt and uncle, Joseph and Phebe Beach Fessenden. You'll catch glimpses of young Phebe long before she took up her pen and began her diary. And you'll be introduced to an unexpected guest. A guest who took me completely by surprise. But, I'll let you discover her for yourself.

In the writing of Book Two, I was supported in my research by Ned Allen at the Bridgton Historical Society, by Kathleen Forsythe Vincent, and by the staff at Bowdoin College George Mitchell Special Collections Library. Cynthia Grimm, "The Comma-dore," served again in the capacity of editor, tackling the very challenging task of editing not just my writing, but also that of Joseph and Phebe Fessenden. She also served as First Reader and Number One Cheerleader.

My biggest thank you goes to all the readers who embraced Book One and eagerly asked when Book Two would be done. Knowing an audience was eagerly waiting helped keep the book on schedule. The wait is over. Dive right in.

With sincere gratitude,

Caroline Grimm

Lark's Haven

Bridgton, Maine

2014

Caroline D. Grimm

The Road to Freedom

June 1851

The last face she saw as they pulled the cover over the wagon was the kind face of the black preacher. His was the last voice she heard as he said, "Go with God, Sister." Tucked into a cozy nest in the center of the wagon, surrounded by casks of ale and wine, she let the rocking of the wagon lull her to sleep.

The wagon traveled the rough roads along the western shore of the great lake they called Sebago. Mathilde slept on, exhausted by her perilous journey. The two men on the wagon bench, one black, one white, kept careful watch of the road, determined to safely deliver their cargo. The Fugitive Slave laws turned some men into money-grubbing opportunists. A slave fresh from the South could bring a tidy sum in hard cash.

The men exchanged a few commonplaces about crops and the vagaries of Maine weather, but both were too intent on reaching their destination to be bothered with much conversation.

As the noon sun rode high in the sky, Mathilde stirred in the dusty, stifling heat beneath the rough burlap covering. For a moment, she could not remember where she was and panic swept through her thin frame. Hearing the sound of the men's voices, she settled again. These men spoke with the clipped brusqueness of the North rather than the slow cadence of the South. "Safe," she thought, but still she could not believe it. She had not felt truly safe since she was a babe in her mother's arms.

She had the misfortune to be too pretty, like her mother. Well-formed with café au lait skin. Her blue eyes told the rest of the story of her parentage. Massa increased his wealth by home-growing more slaves. Young Massa followed in his father's footsteps. He caught his half-sister alone behind the tobacco-drying shed and used her cruelly. That night, she ran.

Huddled in the wagon, Mathilde heard a change in the voices of the men. Guarded and quiet on the wagon ride, now they became boisterous and jovial as the wagon rolled to a stop. She heard a third voice join them. "'Bout time you got here. We're down to our last barrel of ale. Can't have our travelers being thirsty."

"Sorry 'bout that, Sam," spoke the man on the wagon. "Ran into a delay on the road."

"Well, get the wagon in the barn, and we'll get this delivery unloaded so's you can head on back to Portland."

Mathilde made herself as small as she could, not knowing if the new man was friend or foe. The men kept up their boisterous joking while they unloaded the casks from the back of the wagon. The black man from the wagon leaned down and softly said, "You safe, Sister, you in good hands." He helped her climb stiffly down from the wagon. She looked fearfully about the barn. The black man took her gently by the elbow and led her to a trap door in the floor. "You sleep safe here tonight," he said. Opening the trap door, he helped Mathilde descend the ladder into the darkness. She heard the trap door close, and she heard the heavy casks being dragged over the top of the door. Alone in the darkness, she finally allowed herself to weep.

Beach Home

Canaan, Vermont

August, 1813

Samuel Beach caught his wife's eye across the crowded table of jostling offspring. He held her gaze warmly, marveling again at how the loveliness of her smile still stirred him, even after eighteen years of marriage and eleven children. He still recalled the day Mary Bailey, his Pretty Polly, agreed to marry him. He was a big-footed country boy and awkward. Still, she must have seen something special in him. Their love had created this fine quiver of children currently creating chaos at the breakfast table.

Sam, Jr. looked and acted just like his father at the same age. Full of plans and schemes, young Sam was anxious to join the Navy to avenge the American losses in Mr. Madison's War. He was once again regaling his siblings with the tale of Old Ironsides defeating the British ship H.M.S. Guerriere. He chafed at his father's insistence that at age twelve he was far too young to join the Navy.

Samuel looked back at his wife. She was looking tired this morning. The heart-wrenching loss of their newborn twins had stolen the roses from her cheeks. Those sweet, tiny babes, their third set of twins, had lived only twelve hours. Polly was inconsolable. She wept so brokenheartedly over their loss. Dear little Elias and Nathaniel. For two weeks she was not able to rise from her bed and care for her children and her busy household.

Samuel and the oldest girls at home, his twin darlings, Martha and Mary, had shouldered the burden as best they could. At fourteen, the girls were old enough to care for the younger children and get the most necessary work done. They were good, biddable girls, a tribute to their mother's training. Still, Samuel knew his Polly was missing their eldest daughter's capable help. Phebe was away at school in Fryeburg, Maine being trained as a teacher. Spirited Abigail, at age ten, strove to keep tabs on her younger brothers, although Isaac and Israel, at eight years old, resented her bossiness. The little boys Thomas, age 5 and Sargent, age 2 were good sturdy boys used to riding the wake of the older children. They were a sight to warm a father's heart as they clustered around the long, trestle table.

Rising from that table, Samuel said, "With all these hungry mouths to feed, I'd best be getting to work." Turning to his wife, he said, "We're going to work on the dam site on the Canada side. I'll be gone a few days but don't fret. I'll come home as soon as possible." He kissed her on the cheek and squeezed her elbow.

"Say goodbye to your father," Polly told her boisterous brood. "Then, it's time for you all to go to school so that little Sargent and I can get some rest." Samuel heard their groans as he headed out the door smiling.

Samuel stopped at his younger brother's house. Heman Beach had the wagon loaded and the horses hitched and ready. The oxen they needed for the heavy work were yoked and lashed to the back of the wagon. "All ready?" asked Samuel.

"No thanks to you, Brother," Heman replied, grinning. "Too busy kissing your wife again, I suppose."

Samuel slapped him on the back saying, "Envy becomes thee not, Brother." Laughing, they climbed into the wagon and set off for the border.

As the wagon full of tools and supplies jounced along, Heman asked if Samuel had remembered the paperwork for the border crossing. "Judge Ingham signed it for me yesterday. It's there in my satchel." The war with the British had made trade and travel across the Canadian border far more difficult. With the border just three miles from home, it cut into the Beach family's income by restricting trade. It also made working on the Beach mill more difficult, as well. The influx of British soldiers just over the border made smuggling a lucrative business. The British paid in hard coin, and the army needed a constant influx of beef, flour, and ale.

At the border crossing, customs man John Dennet inspected the paperwork, took a cursory look into the wagon, and waved the brothers on through. After moving on, Samuel looked at his brother and said, "Dennet is still angry with me over that tax matter."

Heman nodded and said, "I don't know why you want to be mixed up in town politics like you are. I'd think you'd have enough to do without filling every office, too."

"The town needs solid citizens to look after its affairs."

"I suppose," replied his brother.

The two men bantered back and forth while the wagon rolled along. Samuel talked about the fabrics he was wanting to buy for his pretty girls. "I like to see my girls dressed well and prosperously. With this damned war, it makes it harder to get quality goods."

Heman spoke vehemently against the embargo that made trading with other countries a treasonous act. "It makes no sense for us not to trade with our Canadian neighbors. Madison's got no horse sense at all. It's no wonder everyone ignores the embargo. The swells in Washington are out of touch with what's going on in our part of the country."

Samuel replied, "Well, one good thing has come out of it. We can get English goods cheaper in Canaan than we can coming off the ships in Portland. I got the girls some fine muslins from Scotland and some excellent spider-spun silk from Madagascar. Mary and Martha were well pleased. I'm sending some to Phebe in Fryeburg. I can't have my girl looking like a poor church mouse at that fancy academy she goes to."

About noon, the brothers arrived at their mill. They unhitched the oxen and began unloading the lumber and supplies for the dam. They worked steadily until sundown, then set up camp for the night. For three days, they labored building the dam. Then, they loaded up the wagon and hitched the horses to head back home. At the border crossing, Dennet inspected the wagon and asked about the oxen that were not returning with them. Samuel replied, "We left them with a neighbor."

Dennet looked suspicious. "You better not a sold 'em to the British, or there'll trouble for you," he growled. The Beach brothers were tight-lipped as they moved the wagon forward.

On arriving home, Samuel was greeted exuberantly by his children. They came at him from all sides, asking questions, telling tales, and vying for his attention. Laughing, he held up his hands, saying, "We should send you children to fight the British. They'd surrender in no time." Stepping past them all, he reached his arms out for his Polly, pulling her into a tender embrace. "Any trouble while I was gone?" he asked her.

"All is well," she replied, "Any trouble at the border?" she whispered.

"Dennet is suspicious," he told her quietly, "But all is well."

Two days passed and on a steaming hot August night, Samuel and Polly were awakened by the fearful screaming of eight-year-old Isaac. Racing to his bed, they found him sitting up, raving in delirium and burning with fever. Frantically, they sought to calm him, cool him, and comfort him. All night long, he raved and wandered in his mind. They feared he would not see another morning. Screaming as though possessed, his small frame thrashing about, their dear little Isaac was held fast in the wicked arms of some dread illness.

Polly kept up an unceasing prayer all through the long night. To lose another within less than a month of losing her newborns would be more than she could bear. Mary and Martha took turns comforting the younger children and fetching cool water and clean cloths, while Samuel tried to keep his son from hurting himself as he thrashed and jerked with convulsions. Hours passed in an unwaking nightmare until seven days were gone, and at last Isaac's fever broke. As Isaac fell into a deep, healing sleep, Polly wept with relief. Samuel, exhausted from a week of trying to keep the life spirit in his son, held her, murmuring endearments while shedding his own thankful tears.

The next day, Martha fell ill. And almost immediately, Abigail and little Sargent came down with the same fever. For another week Polly and Samuel went from one bed to the next, desperately trying to save their children. Mary took charge of Isaac's care, helping him recover and build his strength. Young Sam and Israel shouldered the heavy chores with help from their uncle. The house was filled with the sounds of three raving fever victims, the petulant cries of a boy weakened by illness, and the low, urgent demands from the sick rooms.

By the grace of God, all the children survived. The household fell silent as the beleaguered family dropped into an exhausted sleep. In just five dark, terrifying weeks, they had lost two babies and nearly lost four more. Surely, God in his mercy and goodness would spare them any more grief.

Bright and early, on the morning of October 9th, with his family on the mend, Samuel and Heman Beach loaded the wagon for another trip to their mill across the Canadian border. Walking behind the wagon was a new yoke of oxen. With Judge Ingham's signed paperwork in hand, the brothers reached the border where Dennet was once again on customs duty. "That don't look like the same yoke of oxen ya had last time," said Dennet with his eyes squinted in suspicion.

"They look the same to me," Samuel replied, affably. Dennet waved the wagon through but stood watching it as it rolled down the road until it disappeared in a cloud of dust.

The Beach brothers set up camp as before and went to work on the dam. With the oxen doing the heavy pulling, work moved along well, and Samuel and Heman thought to finish the dam on this trip. On the third day, they were surprised to see Dennet ride up with Judge Ingham and three others. Samuel walked up to the men and said, "Is there a problem, gentlemen?"

"Quite so," replied the judge. "Your paperwork is expiring, and you must return across the border."

"We're nearly done here," Samuel replied. "Might we get an extension of another day so we can finish the dam?"

"I'm sorry, you need to return immediately. Dennet here says you plan to sell your oxen to the British while you're here."

"What?! We have no plans to sell the oxen!" Samuel

exclaimed.

Dennet spoke up saying, "Seems like ever' time you come over here to work on your dam, you come back without yer oxen."

"That is an untruth, Sir! Are you accusing me of treason?!"

"I know what I know," was Dennet's angry reply. Seeing no other choice, Samuel and Heman loaded the wagon. Samuel took the small whip from his brother's hand, and turned his oxen to drive them home. As he did, Dennet fired his musket and Samuel Beach crumpled to the ground.

Fryeburg, Maine

October 1813

Phebe Beach woke up with a smile on her face in the bright sunny room she shared with her dear cousin, Mary Ann. It felt good, good, good to wake up with no cares in the world. She lay in bed for a few extra luxurious moments of ease. Her Aunt Abigail Bradley and her kind husband Uncle Robert had welcomed her with open arms when her father brought her from Canaan. "Now, Phebe," Aunt Abigail had told her, "We want you to leave all your worries behind you. You need only pay attention to your schooling here."

It was a relief to Phebe. From the age of three she'd been mother's little helper. She loved her younger brothers and sisters dearly. She learned from an early age to dress, bathe, and feed them. She sang lullabies, told stories, and soothed hurts. She loved the solid feel of them when she held them close. To watch them learn to walk and talk and see their spirits grow was a deep pleasure for her. But, at sixteen, she longed to try her own wings.

Mama and Father had said they could not spare her, especially with another baby on the way, but Phebe wanted more schooling. She yearned for it as some girls yearn for new dresses. She longed to teach, to instruct a classroom of children much as she taught her own brothers and sisters. It was work she felt called to do. Father, at last, decided that sending Phebe to school in Fryeburg was the best choice. With Mary and Martha old enough to take on more of the household responsibilities, Phebe got her chance for more schooling. She was well on her way to realizing her dream of becoming a teacher.

Since coming to Fryeburg, she'd made fast friends with so many cousins and schoolmates. Every day brought some new outing or party. Phebe's health, always delicate, improved with the plentiful food and rest her aunt insisted upon. For Phebe, it was a time of new, young life and intellectual discovery. It was also a time for another type of discovery. The young men at the Academy were drawn to Phebe's fresh-faced beauty. And because she was "from away," she was a new and interesting discovery for them. Her father had grown concerned after reading her letters home. So full were her letters of parties and social gatherings and young men, he grew concerned for her virtue. Ever a caring and protective father, he wrote her cautioning her against the evils she might fall prey to with no father near to guard her. She kept his letters close by, re-reading them whenever she felt homesick.

O, my dear child,

I think of you and miss you each and every day. I worry to have you so far away from my protection. I suppose you are surrounded with friends. You have a tender and loving aunt and a kind and affectionate uncle who, we have no doubt, will do everything they can for your good. You have, no doubt, pleasant and agreeable neighbours who will respect you. You live in a fine house in a pleasant village surrounded with harvest fields and pleasant meadows. All is lovely and gay. But your little soul has not yet been stung. Your lucid eyes have not yet seen what I am about to tell you.

There are holes and dens in Fryeburg, too. Devils and angry dragons inhabit them. Vipers and adders live there. O, beware, my little child, beware, lest they fall upon you and devour you. There are wolves, too, that wear sheeps' clothing. They will approach you unawares. You will think that they are lambs. They will fawn round you with false prettiness, with flattering words of wily lies. Beware, o my child, beware. Satan, you recollect, beguiled Eve. You, too, may be deceived. Their wool, which looks so sleek and smooth, is all dog's hair. Their words are barbed darts. They have stings about them which will pierce your heart and leave a mortal wound. Such, my child, is wicked man, and worse things, too, if it could be described.

It may have seemed to you that your parents have wanted to keep them from you, but our knowledge and experience in life hath taught us to be alarmed for you. We are alarmed. We tremble lest you should fall prey to the wickedness of man. We want to have you remember us and take care of yourself for us. You must not forget to be always at home with your aunt at all times when the sun is set. You perhaps have thought us a little hard at our opposing your going to balls and places of gaiety and amusement. We would explain ourselves.

The company has never been an objection with us, but it is the time they occupy, the night. We have been afraid to have you out of our sight in the dark lest some beast of prey should fall upon you and devour you. We have no objection to your going to respectable balls in the day time, but it must always be understood that you are to be returned to your aunt by sunset.

This is my command and should anybody attempt to persuade you to break it, you must, like a little woman, expostulate with them. You must tell them that you have the commands of a father upon you which you cannot, you dare not, and that you will not disobey. If you cannot prevail upon your partner by soft and generous expostulations, and by informing him, whomever he may be, that it is the solemn injunctions of a father's command that you wish to obey, you must apply to some respectable young lady, and make known your situation to her, and request her to intercede with some gentleman to conduct you home, and never be caught in company again with a man who would compel you to break your father's commands. Such men are your enemies.

Again, Phebe, I tell you beware of that man who wishes to pursue his affections any farther than will damage your honour. You must let such ministers of corruption understand that you are not at liberty to receive a dishonourable proposition from any man. Reflect for a moment with me, Phebe, on this matter. See if I am correct.

Would you suppose that if any person had a design upon ending your life, you would flee them as you would a serpent? Be assured that that person, under whatever pretence, who wishes to rob you of your honour is worse than a murderer. Better would that wretch serve you and me and my family should he pierce your heart with a sword than to commit a depredation upon your chastity. I have dealt plain and familiarly with you, Phebe. I think you cannot mistake me.

I shall now after again committing you to your uncle and aunt's care, commit them and you into the hands of that God who is alone able to keep you from all dangers and misfortunes. You

*must in a very respectful manner remember me to your uncle and
aunt Bradley and to all the family connections. Tell them I shall
write to them the next opportunity. Your mother will write to you. I
must conclude my long letters, my dear child, by subscribing
myself,*

Your father and friend,

Samuel Beach

The dear man went to great lengths to counsel her, to ensure she
always felt her father's care and protection, though she was far
from home. She might have laughed about the letter with her
friends, but she could not bring herself to. This was her own dear
father's way of protecting her, and she treasured his care and
concern.

She heeded her father's warnings, as a good girl should. With
all the single gentlemen at the Academy, Phebe certainly could
have had her choice. But, in her eyes, only one gentleman stood
out. Joe Fessenden. Tall and courtly with kind blue eyes and a
gentle wit. He was the son of Fryeburg's first pastor. His father had
died when Joe was just thirteen. Joe had known great loss already
in his young life. Five years before his father died, he lost his older
brother Caleb at the age of nineteen, and just six weeks after his
father passed away, his seventeen-year-old sister died, too.

Joe understood the uncertainties of life. He was a good
student, working hard to make something of himself. He had a
bright future, planning to continue his education. He had his sights
set on Bowdoin College and a career in law. He hoped to join his
brother Samuel in his law practice. Dear man, he'd been so kind to
her when she'd received news of the loss of her newborn brothers.

His seriousness about school did not keep him from enjoying
the lighter side of life. He was a great favorite at dances and on

outings. Just last week, a group of friends from school had gone to climb Jockey Cap Mountain to see the view from the top. The fall leaves had not turned yet, waiting for a strong frost to reach their peak of glory. Joe managed to get Phebe away from the group for a talk. He asked her about her dreams for her life. She told him she wanted more than anything to keep school for a few years. After that, she wanted to marry and have as many children as God would give her. Joe was quite taken with her, she was certain. And for her part, she could see no better future than having a fine young man like Joe as her life mate. She lay in bed for a few extra moments of dreaming of what the future might hold.

Rising blithely from her bed, she dressed carefully for the day, fixing her hair in the new attractive way her cousins had devised for her. Grabbing up her school books, she ran lightly down the stairs to enjoy breakfast in the sunny kitchen. Calling out a cheery good morning, she was taken aback by the seriousness of her Uncle's face, and she saw that Aunt Abigail had been crying. "What is it? What's happened?"

Uncle Robert held out his hand to her and said, "Sit down, my dear. I'm afraid I have some very bad news for you."

Sitting slowly down, she asked almost in a whisper, "Is it Mother? Is Mother alright?" Aunt Abby started to sob.

Uncle Robert held her hand tighter. "No, dear, it's your father. He's been shot. I'm so sorry to tell you he died on Saturday."

"Oh, my dear Father! My mother! My poor family!" Phebe broke down sobbing. Aunt Abigail held her in her arms, and they both wept for the terrible loss and the fatherless children. "I must go home at once," she sobbed.

"We leave today," said Uncle Robert patting her arm. "Mary Ann will help you pack."

On the long journey home, Phebe was withdrawn and worried. What would become of her family now without her father to support them? As the oldest child she felt the weight of the responsibility settle hard upon her slender shoulders. Her mother was already burdened with the care and work of all those children. Her health had not yet revived after Elias and Nathaniel were born and so sadly died less than three months ago. She wept for her sweet sisters and dear brothers who would grow up without the loving care of a father. She wept for little Sargent and Tommy who would grow up without truly knowing their father. And she wept for young Sam, who at twelve was not ready for the burden of being the man of the house. It all seemed to fall back on her shoulders as the eldest child. It was up to her to fill the gaping hole left by her father's death. To be a strong shoulder for her mother, to be a provider for her family, and to make certain the children were raised in a way to make their father proud.

When the wagon pulled into the dooryard of her home, she ran into the house, calling for her mother. The usual apple-pie order was displaced by dirty dishes in the sink and a house in disarray. Sargent was sitting under the table looking forlorn and covered with mud. Tommy was staring out the window. Mary and Martha were trying to pull together a meal for the grieving family. Abigail was sunk in gloom.

Putting her own grief aside, Phebe took charge. Putting on a clean apron, she coaxed Abigail to take charge of cleaning up Sargent. She put Tommy on a chair to help her with dishes. She gave an encouraging look to Mary and Martha who both looked relieved at having their sister's steadying presence. As Phebe and her young charges worked to stabilize the household, her exhausted mother walked through the door. Her poor eyes were swollen from weeping, she had dark circles under her eyes, and she staggered from weariness. "Oh my dear girl, thank you for coming so quickly. I've been lost without you here."

"Oh, Mama, I cannot believe he's gone!" Phebe started to break down, but seeing the exhaustion on her mother's face, she composed herself and briskly said, "Alright, Mama, sit down right here while I make you a cup of tea. You must keep up your strength for the trials ahead."

Just then, Samuel came storming into the house. "Can you believe what they're saying?! It's in the paper that Father was shot for smuggling oxen to the British! It's a damnable lie, and I will not stand by and listen to my father's good name being dragged through the bloody mud!"

"Samuel!" Phebe admonished, "Mind your language in front of the children. You're only making a bad matter worse. Go out to the barn and see to the cows, please!" Samuel was too angry to be calmed. Beneath the anger, Phebe could see the depth of his hurt and fear. Forced to grow up overnight, he was struggling like a newborn colt to get his legs under him. "Samuel, I need your help here. I can't do it alone," she spoke quietly but firmly to him.

He saw how she was working around her own hurt and fear and drew courage from her. He placed a hand on her shoulder and said, "It's good to have you home." He headed to the barn to take care of the heavy chores.

Oh, the grief-filled days that followed! Standing with her family around the yawning grave that would hold her dear father's earthly remains. The pathetic weeping of her mother and the fatherless children. Phebe's young heart broke for her family and for the loss of the father whose love and care she had just begun to truly appreciate. Her seventeenth birthday passed without celebration. She simply could not care about such an insignificant event in the face of such despair. Each day was filled with crushing responsibility. Getting the children up, dressed, fed, and off to school. Distracting little Sargent to give her mother room to grieve the loss of her beloved companion. Finding a little corner of the day to let out some of her own great grief. The days passed one after another in misery and despair.

Dennet was jailed for murder, but it was small compensation for a family that had lost its husband and father, its sole support in the world. Doctor bills from the spotted fever that had so sorely tried her family remained unpaid. Without her father's income, it would not be long before the family faced financial ruin. To watch all that her father had built up drain away was a trial to Phebe. Her father had gone from debtor's prison to building a comfortable life with many small luxuries for his family. Now, they stood on the brink of poverty again because of one callous man's bullet. Phebe could feel her mother's anxiety whenever she walked into a room. What would become of a widow with nine children to raise and no man to earn a living?

In the early morning hours before the family began to stir, Phebe quietly rose and left the chamber she shared with her three young sisters. Taking a bundle of letters with her, she went to the kitchen and stirred up the fire. Sitting in her mother's rocking chair, lovingly made by her father as he had awaited the birth of his first child seventeen years before, Phebe opened her packet of letters. She pulled out the last letter her father had written to her less than a month before he died. Scanning through the letter, she found the passage she was looking for and read her father's spidery handwriting:

How swift the minutes roll. A few days ago, I was young like you. And now my head is gray. I am treading down the hill of life. A few days more and the hand that now wields this pen will be cold as clay. These eyes that trace the path of the quill will be closed. The heart that pours forth these lines will be buried in the grave.

As he wrote those words to her, her father could not have known how true his thoughts ran. He had just a few more days to live before God called him home. A tear ran down her cheek and fell on her father's last words to her. She continued to read.

You have mounted a great stage, Phebe. Act well your part. There, all honour lies. It is said that the travelers are few on wisdom's highway. Be wise, my dear child, to improve time as a talent. Be wise. But be a fool as they call those that follow the Lamb. You recollect that the scriptures say how the preaching of Christ was foolishness to those who were the most learned of polite people in the world. Be wise, my Phebe, to lay up your treasure, as your grandfather used to pray, where moth and dust doth not corrupt.

You, my dear daughter, are at this time just ripening into a life. Vast and unexplored is the field that is opening before you. Strange scenes await us all. Time is big with events which will burst upon you. As you trip it along her highway, new and portentous events await the world, and you, my dear, are one among the myriad thousand of concomitant parts which makes up the great whole. You must take a part in this scene. You must be an actress on the stage. Act well your part.

Your conscience will bear you witness. God has placed in your breast a little compass, sure as the dial which never errs, invariably pointing you in the way which you should go. This, my child, is the finger of God to which, if you are careful to take heed, if you pay strict attention to the bearings and pointings of this compass, if you listen to the warnings and entreaties of the whole spirit, you will be wise and in the right.

Mariners sailing the ocean provide themselves with a compass with which by frequent observations they make their destination. You, dear child, must make frequent observations and pay due attention to your own compass as you float along the ocean of life.

I must break off my letter before it is hardly begun. I intended to have written you a long letter before you returned home. A letter for you to have carried into life with you. A father's fond instructions for you to look back upon if you should live beyond me. But I must be done as it is now almost 11 o'clock and my old eyes are almost blinded with the light of the candle. My child, adieu.

Reading her father's last fond farewell to her brought fresh tears to Phebe's eyes. How like her father to give her one last gift. The final fatherly advice he would ever give her. To be wise, but also foolish, on her pathway through the world. Where she now lacked the protection of a father, she would need more than ever to cling to her faith and to the gentle wisdom of a loving father.

Folding her father's last letter carefully, she rose from the rocking chair and began breakfast preparations, hoping to find some tidbit to tempt her mother's weak appetite. With the household sunk in gloom, her mother burdened with the grief of losing two babes and her husband, and the young ones still weak from the spotted fever and their own grief, Phebe tried to muster up the courage to face another day. How did people survive such tragedies and still keep going? She felt trapped in a cloud of darkness and misery. She felt she must find work soon, or the family would soon be without the basic necessities. If she could find a school to keep, it would at least provide some income. She felt the world weighing down on her young shoulders and wished for a strong arm around her to give her courage. Swiping impatiently at the tears that seemed to roll down her face constantly, she went to wake the children to get them dressed and ready for the day.

Two weeks passed, and for the Beach family, each day seemed an unending monotony of work and grief. Phebe felt she would never again be happy in her time on earth. She diligently wrote to everyone the family knew to help her find a teaching position. The letters she received in reply were filled with compassion for her, her mother, and her family. But every one had the same disappointing news. No positions available. If she did not find work soon, her family would be hungry. The worry was taking its toll. Her face was drawn and pinched and her thin frame had grown gaunt. How could God have so forsaken her and her family?

Phebe sat alone in the cold house staring out the window. Polly Beach had taken her youngest son with her to the store to see if the shopkeeper would extend the family a little more credit. The children were all at school. The floors needed sweeping and the wood box needed filling, but Phebe could not seem to stir herself from her window seat. Dully, she saw a carriage pull up in front of the house. Watching, she saw a young man swing down and head for the door, looking about curiously. Her eyes widened when she realized it was Joe Fessenden coming to the door. What was he doing so far from home? She ran to the door and opened it before he had a chance to knock. "Joe!" she exclaimed.

"Oh, my dear friend," he replied, pulling her into a warm embrace. She clung to him with her head resting on his chest, reveling in the strength and warmth of his arms around her. "Oh, my dear," he said, "What a time you have had." The kindness of his tone released a flood of pent-up emotions, and she found herself sobbing wildly in his arms. He held her while she let loose the grief that had built up in her as she cared for her mother and her family. The grief of a young girl whose father was lost to her forever. The grief of a young woman with the burdens of the world thrust upon her too soon.

Patiently, Joe waited out the storm. When she quieted, he led her to the rocking chair by the hearth. He gave her his handkerchief and put the kettle on for a cup of tea. Phebe gathered herself and took several deep breaths to calm her emotions. Looking up at Joe with a tear-ravaged face, she said, "I apologize for my poor manners in greeting you. It's just that I've been feeling so alone and overwhelmed, and I never thought to see you again."

Joe replied with a grin, "Does this mean you are happy I came?"

Phebe laughed. It was the first time she'd laughed since her last day in Fryeburg. "Oh, so very happy," she replied.

Mrs. Beach came in just then with a small bundle of food. She placed it on the table and turned to greet the visitor. Phebe spoke to her mother saying, "Mama, this is Mr. Joseph Fessenden, my friend from the Academy. Mr. Fessenden, may I present my mother, Mrs. Beach."

"A pleasure, Ma'am. I wish the circumstances of our meeting were happier. I do sincerely grieve with you on your loss."

Mrs. Beach nodded and said, "Won't you please be seated, sir? I see my good daughter has already put the kettle on for tea." Phebe and Joe glanced at each other with a little secret smile. What passed between them would be a personal matter, not shared with any other.

Joe said, "I nearly forgot, Miss Beach, I bring you a letter from your Aunt Abigail in Fryeburg." Reaching into his coat pocket, he retrieved the letter and handed it to Phebe.

Breaking the seal eagerly, she glanced quickly at the contents of the letter. As she read, a smile crossed her face, and she looked to her mother with excitement. "She found me a school! Mama!

She found me a school!"

Just then, the children all rolled in through the door, chattering about their day. They stopped when they saw Joe, looking up at him curiously. Phebe made the introductions, and Joe's natural warmth and curiosity soon won all of the children over. The older girls, Mary and Martha barraged him with questions about what the girls were wearing in Fryeburg. He responded by telling them he was sure he didn't know since he only noticed one girl there. They giggled and looked at Phebe who blushed prettily. Sam quizzed him about news of the war. Abigail tried out her flirting skills on him. The little boys soon had him in a wrestling match on the floor.

For the first time since before all the troubles had besieged the Beach family, laughter rang out in their home and the gloom lifted for a little while. Phebe watched Joe playing with her brothers and sisters. She saw the respect and courtesy he paid to her mother. And she saw the little glances he continually threw her way. She began to believe that, with time, she could once again be happy. At least she could be if she had this man by her side.

Later, Joe and Phebe slipped away from the children for a walk through Canaan. She showed him all the sights the small town could afford. She told him of the circumstances of her father's death. She told of the mill on the Canada side and the trouble caused by the war. Before they returned to the house, Joe took Phebe by the hand in a quiet spot at the edge of the woods. Looking into her eyes, he said, "My dear friend, I hope I am not speaking out of turn, and if I am, I beg your forgiveness. I have deep feelings for you. I am not in a position to ask for your hand as yet. I must attend college before I marry so that I can provide well for my wife. When I finish college, I know not what job I shall have or where I shall live. But, dear friend, I know one thing to be true. I would be honored if so fine a woman as yourself would consent to share her life with me. For my part, I would do any job that would provide well for you and your poor family. I would live anywhere that you could be happy. May I ask you to wait for me? You are too good for me by far, but may I hope?"

Looking up at him, Phebe sighed, "You are my dear friend, and I would be honored if you would hold me in your heart while you are away from me."

Joe looked at her with a mixture of joy and questioning. "May I?" he asked. She replied by tilting up her mouth, and he sealed their pact with a chaste kiss.

Walking back to the house as the sun set, the couple strolled hand in hand speaking of what the future might hold for them. Keeping school in Fryeburg for Phebe and attending college in Brunswick for Joe. Two long years before they could join their lives. A long separation and no certainty that life would spare them long enough to marry. "Life is uncertain, and so it is precious," said Phebe. Joe kissed her hand and held her a little closer as the first star shone in the sky.

A few days after Joe Fessenden departed from Canaan to return to Fryeburg, Polly Beach handed her daughter a letter. Phebe took the letter and tucked it into her apron pocket until she could find a private moment to read it. Later, when the children were gathered around the table working on homework, Phebe went to her room and sat down on the side of the bed she shared with her sisters. Carefully opening the letter, she read:

November 8, 1813

My good girl,

Solitary and alone at the hour of 11 in the evening, I put my pen upon my paper, and in the sincerity of a true and constant friend, communicate my thoughts and feelings to my Phebe. Time with its most rapid, and to me, most dreary wheels, has rolled away one fortnight since I clasped your hand and bade you farewell. Since then, not a day has passed in which I have not been with you in imagination, have not strained you closely to my heart and mingled my tears with yours o'er the grave of your departed Father. In imagination, lowly bending over the coffin of her son, I have seen the tears trickle down the cheeks of your venerable Grandmother. I have heard the plaints and groans of your mother, have seen her turn up her eyes to Heaven, and place her trust in Jesus, who is the husband of the widow, and protector of the orphan.

Often, in the bitterness of sorrow, I exclaim, "O! Thou God of Heaven, how canst thou suffer the bosom of the innocent to be torn by agonizing grief? But again, I say thou art a righteous God; thou dost, tis true, afflict thy creatures, but thou afflictest them for their benefit; thou dost wound them, but thou only woundest to heal again; and thou surely will be the father and defender of my Phebe."

What can I say to console you? Your Father, my Phebe, is now a happy Angel in Heaven; now looks down with complacency upon his child. You have friends who will do all things in their power for the promotion of your happiness. With these considerations, you will receive consolation. Were I to tell you that I am one of these friends, the sincerest of any, I should tell no more than that, which you yourself do know.

With you, the humblest cottage of a shepherd would be for me a happy residence. Without you, the most magnificent palace of a prince would be but a dreary and desolate mansion. Think not I say this for the petty gratification of hearing myself talk, while inwardly I have different thoughts. Neither you, nor any one else has ever known me to assert a lie. As a brother, then, you will not hesitate at all times, to let me know your mind. You are far from me surrounded by murderers and robbers and can, readily, imagine what are my feelings, and how great is my anxiety for you.

If you consider me as a brother, for so you have called me, and so indeed I am, I will ask what brother is there, who unless callous and hardened to the feelings of nature, would not, when his sister is absent from him encompassed by monsters—monsters, who have taken from her the kindest and dearest of Fathers, who have deprived the world of one of its brightest ornaments—rush forward to protect her, and with one hand take her to his bosom, and with the other wield his sword like a giant in her defence? So will I, at all times, with my life and property be your guardian. Yes, though ten thousand swords are pointed at my breast and though my heart strings crack from their strokes, yet in the convulsive grasp of death, I will hold you fast and bid defiance to the wretch who may dare to harm you.

I have many things to tell you and shall, I hope, with your permission, ere long make you a visit, when I think I can make you a new proposal which you will approve and will I think be advantageous to us both. I shall wait with impatience for your answer to my letter in which you will not fail to let me know every particular relative to your situation.

Night wanes swiftly. Tis now past three in the morning, and all those around me are still and silent. The guardian Angel of Heaven, I trust, has shadowed his wings over you and weighed down your eyelids in gentle repose and will awake you to a pleasant morning. It will be useless for me to make any excuses for the many errors in my letter. It is going to my Phebe, and she will forgive them. And now I will bid you good night with the assurance that though you should discard me and should find another, who perhaps, may be more worthy of you, yet that you may enjoy not only all the blessings and care which this life can afford, but that at your death you may have an inheritance in Heaven incorruptible, undefiled and that fadeth not away shall ever be the prayer of your friend,

Joseph P. Fessenden

Phebe held Joe's letter close to her heart, her hands lovingly touching the pages that his hand had touched. She thought of him sitting at his desk writing deep into the night to bring her comfort. "This is the man for me; the man I will marry," she whispered. She tucked the letter back into her apron pocket and went to help her brothers and sisters with their studies. That night, she kissed the letter and slid it under her pillow when her sisters were not looking. She slept, content knowing that somewhere under the same moon, her love was thinking of her and wishing her well.

Polly Beach was pressed hard by the shopkeeper to pay at least a portion of her bill. He would give her no more credit until the bill was paid. She stopped at her brother-in-law Heman's house in shame to ask if he could loan her the money. Heman's business had suffered from the loss of Samuel, as well. He said he had no hard cash to spare. In despair, Polly went home empty-handed. She knew the family was getting closer to the keen edge of hunger every day. Soon, Phebe would leave for her teaching position in Fryeburg, but that did not provide the food needed for this day.

She entered the house with despair written on her drawn face. Phebe looked up from the washtub where she was scrubbing the girls' small clothes. "Mama, what is it?" she cried, "Has something else happened?"

"No, daughter, nothing new. I have reached the end of our money, and I do not know where to turn. I'm sorry to burden you so, dear, but I cannot raise the money to pay the grocery bill, the doctor needs to be paid still, and the taxes are due. I am at the very end of my wits." With that, she slumped into the rocking chair and put her apron over her face.

Phebe stood with her arms in the wash basin, continuing to scrub her sisters' clothes. She looked upon her mother's bent head, the desperation of their circumstances stretched out before them. How would they feed the children? Surely there must be some way for her to earn some money to help out. If only her school had started sooner.

Phebe dried her arms and hands on cotton dish cloth. She stepped over to her mother and, kneeling beside her, she wrapped her arms around the grieving woman. "Mama, don't fret so. Surely, we will find our way through this darkness. Surely, we will."

Polly lifted her head and looked into the frightened eyes of her eldest daughter. "Yes, my dear," she said, "We must have faith. God will not abandon us now."

That evening, Phebe sat down to write to her Aunt Bradley in Fryeburg. She poured her lonely heart out to that good woman, knowing she would find a willing ear. She told it all. The fear of hunger at the door. The grief of her family. The desperation of their situation. And her own despair and the great weight she felt on her own shoulders. The letter relieved her a bit of her worries as talking always did. But it still did not pay the grocer's bill or the doctor's bill.

A few days after she sent the letter, she received one from Joe. Where his last letter was received with great joy, this one was received indifferently, sunk as she was in abject misery. She sat at the kitchen table and stared at the letter for a few moments. Then, breaking the seal, she read:

November 15, 1813

My good Phebe,

I wrote you a letter or, rather, something in the shape of a letter a short time since and sent it by mail. Thinking it possible that it may miscarry or be delayed and having no opportunity of sending one in safety by the hand of your cousin, I cannot, I will not, let it pass without again addressing thee. The sad vicissitude of fortune which has lately overwhelmed you with sorrow, in the death of a dear and affectionate parent, will, I fear, soon lay your head as lowly as his, unless you summon that Christian fortitude— that resignation to the will of Heaven, which protects, supports, and defends the Disciples of Christ.

I was told by your Aunt that in a letter you stated that your health was bad, that life was no longer dear, and that melancholy and despair seemed to be almost your only companions. This, my Phebe, will never do. The interest I take in your welfare, and the anxiety I feel when you are in distress, prompts me to beg that you would listen for a moment while I exert my feeble abilities in attempting to impress deeply upon your mind the necessity of your being particularly cautious of your health.

This world, 'tis true, and its enjoyments are not worth possessing. But God in his Providence has placed us here. Here, to the utmost of our ability, we are to perform that part, which he, in his wisdom, may allot us. Here, we are to meet adversity and stem the torment of affliction. Here, with resolution, which neither the vile of this world can shake nor the demons of Hell overturn, we are to oppose everything bad and, so far as we are able, advance the cause of our Redeemer.

And you must remember, too, that you are to be, with the assistance of Heaven, the prop and support of the declining years of your mother. You, by your example and instructions, are to assist in training up your younger brothers and sisters and fitting them to be useful in their day and generation. Will you then suffer your health to decay, Phebe, by indulging in unavailing woe? I know you will not.

The ways of Providence are indeed dark and intricate but intended in righteousness. Courage, then, and fear not. God will protect you and your family and shield you from harm. I was once young and am now old said the Prophet; yet have I never known the righteous forsaken or their seed begging their bread. Can you then fear? Certainly not. The land which has enveloped your youth in sadness will one day be succeeded by a bright and lucid sunshine.

If I could render you any assistance, on the swiftest wings would I fly to do it. You know very well that my life, my all are chained to your direction. It would be the delight of my soul to guard and defend you, to be a son indeed to your good mother and a kind and affectionate brother to her children. I hope and trust and long that I shall be all of these things, though I fear I am unworthy. Whether you, my good girl, cast one thought upon me or not, my attachment for you will never be shaken. I will ever do all things in my power for the promotion of your happiness. You know me and cannot mistake my character. However, I can only say that whatever I am, Heaven knows the sincerity of my heart.

Here I will stop for I have already written enough to tire your patience in the reading it. Be my friend still, Phebe, and take good care of your health. Write me. Fail not and write me, and let me know your thoughts and feelings toward me.

I am thy friend, thy brother, in sincerity, and will remain so until death. Joe P. Fessenden

She carefully refolded Joseph's letter and placed it listlessly in her apron pocket. She could not find the joy she once felt, and truthfully, his words hurt her, like little stinging cuts to her heart. Did he not understand? She wanted to feel better. She wanted to be cheerful. She wanted to lift herself up out of her despair. But wanting to, and doing so seemed completely unrelated in her low frame of mind. She knew he meant well. This was Joseph after all. He ever did mean well. It was one of the reasons she felt so warmly toward him. Still, she felt trapped in her melancholy, suffocated and adrift in despair. With problem after problem needing to be faced every day, life had become a pathway of jagged, unrelenting stones. Phebe squared her shoulders, heaved one self-pitying sigh, and turned her hand to her next household task.

Fryeburg, Maine

December 1813

The sound of carriage wheels on the road outside her comfortable home brought Abigail Bradley running to fling wide the door in warm welcome. As the carriage came to a stop, she saw the pale face of her beloved niece looking toward her. "Phebe, dear girl," Aunt exclaimed, "Come out of that carriage this instant." Phebe climbed out of the carriage and into Aunt's warm embrace. "Come inside. You must be half frozen." With their arms entwined, the two women stepped through the doorway and into the warmth of the front parlor.

"My dear, dear girl," Aunt gushed. "How we have missed your sweet face. And oh, what a trial you have been through. You are all together too thin. We must fatten you before you start school." Aunt bustled about taking Phebe's cloak and mittens. Phebe stood docile under her aunt's ministrations. Aunt prattled on about all the new happenings in Fryeburg: marriages, new babies, and departed souls. Finally, she slowed down enough to glance at Phebe. "My dear, you are not well. And here I am running on. Come sit down by the fire. Let me fetch you some tea." She bustled off to the kitchen to put the kettle on the stove. Phebe sank down into the nearest chair.

For two weeks, she had been marshalling her strength and will for the journey back to Fryeburg. With only a few days left before the winter term began, she struggled to find the strength she would need to begin keeping school. She had to find a way. Her family was relying on her for support. She hoped a few days in her aunt's care, far from the worries of home, would help build up her strength. That night, tucked up in her old room with her cousin Mary Ann in the bed next to her, she fell into the first restful sleep she had had since the last time she had slept in that bed. Waking in the morning, she found her spirit a bit lighter. Over breakfast, she found herself smiling over Mary Ann's school stories. A brisk walk to the village to run an errand for Aunt brought some color to her cheeks. Within a couple of days, she surprised herself by laughing out loud at the antics of Mary Ann's orange kitten.

When the first day of the winter term arrived, Phebe rose up early and dressed carefully. The old familiar first day of school jitters fluttered her stomach, this term even more so. This would be her first day at the front of the school room. She carefully tucked her hair into a tight bun and smoothed back the tendrils that longed to escape. When she was satisfied that she looked the part of a proper school marm, she solemnly descended the stairs to the kitchen for breakfast. When Aunt saw her, she exclaimed, "Well, I declare! If it isn't Miss Beach, the school teacher. My dear, you look wonderful!" Phebe blushed with the compliment and quietly took her place at the table.

Uncle took her by carriage to the little village school. Tightly grasping the straps of her book satchel, she barely spoke on the trip, too nervous by far for idle chatter. Stopping at the steps of the school, Uncle Robert tipped his hat to her and said, "You'll do just fine, dear. I will pick you up when school lets out for the day." Phebe nodded her head and gave him half a smile.

Climbing down, she stiffly walked to the school, relieved that none of her students had arrived yet. She walked up the stairs and opened the door. She stood in the doorway for a moment before moving down the aisle. At the front of the classroom, she turned, standing behind the desk, looking out at the empty benches. Soon, those benches would be filled with squirming boys and giggling girls, all looking at her curiously—looking to her to guide their education.

For a moment, she felt her knees turn to water. She was barely older than some of her pupils, not long out of school herself. Then, she thought of her young brothers and sisters sitting around the kitchen table struggling as they learned to read and cipher. These children were surely just like her own brood. Each one needing her help, her guidance, her encouragement. She set about lighting a fire in the stove and making the school room warm and inviting for the children. Her children. It had a comforting sound to it. Moments later, she stood at the door ringing the hand bell and welcoming her pupils in the door with a gracious smile.

The first week of the school term passed quickly. When Friday rolled around and Phebe dismissed her school for the weekend, she looked about the school room and wondered how it had gotten so disheveled in just a few days. She began stacking books and tidying up, getting everything in readiness for Monday morning. As she was erasing the chalkboard, she felt a cold breeze as the door opened, and she heard a polite cough from the doorway. She said, "I'm nearly done, Uncle, I'll be right there." Turning to glance at him, she was surprised to see not her uncle, but Joe Fessenden standing in the doorway. He was gazing at her with a mixture of pleasure and nervousness. They had not seen each other for months. She had not answered his last letter. She had never thought to see him again, too deep in her sorrows to think of her own heart. And yet, there he was. Her heart leapt in remembered joy. Her dear friend. Her Joseph.

Awkwardly, they faced each other. Neither sure enough to speak the first word, make the first move. Joe cleared his throat nervously. Phebe remembered her manners and walked gracefully toward him with her hand outstretched, "Joseph, this is an unexpected pleasure. Please do come in."

He twisted his hat in his hands, clearly unsure of himself. "The pleasure is mine, Phebe." He shuffled his feet and looked around the room. They both started to speak at once. He bowed his head to her in deference, "My apologies. You were saying?"

"No, no, please," she replied. Clearing his throat and swallowing hard, Joseph said, "I had heard of your coming and thought to pay you a visit. I hope I am not overstepping my welcome."

"Not at all, Joseph, I am happy to see you."

"How are you," he asked, "And your mother and the children? How fare they?" he inquired. Feeling herself on safer ground in discussing her family, she related the news from home. They worked through the stiffness of their greeting, looking for the old familiarity they had shared before the terrible trials. Settling into each other's presence, their reserve began to wear away. Soon they were back to the Phebe and Joe of their school days.

After a time, Joseph grew serious again. "Phebe, I fear I offended you with my last letter. I did mean you no ill will. My concern for you was great. Did I overstep my bounds? Were you troubled by my words? Why did you not respond? I have been on pins and needles hoping to hear from you!"

Phebe glanced down at the school room floor. Tears welled up in her eyes. She could not respond. Watching her, reading her mood, Joseph reached out a hand and gently cupped her chin. "My dear girl, I did not mean to trouble you." She looked up at him with brimming eyes. "Can you tell me what troubles you, my dear? I would give all I have to see you smile."

Phebe drew in a shuddering breath and began to cry in earnest. Joseph pulled her to his chest, holding her until the worst of the storm passed. She dabbed at her face with her handkerchief, saying, "I am so sorry. I don't know what came over me. Please do pardon me."

With deep kindness, Joseph replied, "Now, tell me, Phebe, if you can, what troubles you?" She looked up at him with her eyes still damp and her face tear-stained. "I could not write to you; I was too low. I did not want to cause you worry. And then, it felt like I would never feel better, and I could not burden you with my troubles any more. I thought it best to let the matter rest."

Joseph looked sadly at Phebe. "Do you not know? Do you not know the regard I have for you? I would gladly bear all your troubles for you if I could. But how can I help you if you don't let me know how it is with you? You must always tell me so I can help you or if not help you, support you with prayer and good words. Phebe, if I could speak my heart right now I would. But I have no right until I am through with school. Still you must know how I feel. Can you not read my thoughts and feel what I feel for you?"

Phebe stared hard into Joseph's blue eyes. In those eyes, she saw concern and kindness and something else. A warmth that could not be denied. A growing warmth that she felt, too. They stood like that, staring into each other's eyes. Lost in this sweet emotion, this sweet rush. Their reverie was broken by the sound of the door opening. Uncle Robert, come to fetch her home, glanced at the couple with a knowing smile and said, "I can see my services are not needed this afternoon. Mr. Fessenden, I presume my niece will arrive safely and promptly home?"

Joseph blushed and, without taking his eyes off Phebe, said, "Squire Bradley, you may rest assured she will come to no harm in my care."

For the remainder of the school term, Phebe and Joseph spent as much time together as possible. They threw themselves into the social life of the village, parties and picnics, balls and fetes. At every possible chance, Joseph took Phebe by the hand and whisked her away from the careful eyes of the chaperones. She scolded him, saying, "Joseph! It isn't proper!" all the while giggling and blushing as he stole a kiss or wrapped his solid arms around her.

Time passes too soon for lovers. The school term ended, and Phebe was needed at home to give her poor mother a respite from her cares. Joseph paid a formal call on Phebe, standing stiffly in her Aunt's best parlor. He looked sadly down into Phebe's eyes. "My dear girl, what shall I do without you? It may be months before we see each other again. I cannot bear to see you go. If I could only speak my heart to you now! But I must go to college. I promised my father before he died that I would. And my brother, Sam, is helping me, so I must go. I ask you to please consider waiting for me. Will you do that for me, Phebe? Will you?"

He looked at her with such longing and worry that she felt her eyes well up at his distress. "Oh, Joe, I cannot make you any promises yet. I must take care of my family. I do wish we could be together always, but I must help my mother and the children. Say you understand, please, Joe?"

Joseph bowed his head for a moment, struggling to contain his emotions. "My girl, I do understand, and I wish I could do more to help your family. I feel so strongly for them all. Will you at least promise to write to me always and tell me just what you are thinking? I can bear the waiting if I know you are thinking of me fondly and often."

"Joe, I promise I will write to you always and tell you how I am feeling." With that, he took her hand and gently kissed it, holding it to his cheek while he held her gaze in his. Then, clasping her tightly to his chest, he dropped one last kiss on her hair and let her go. She left him with tears in her eyes, torn between staying with him and going to the family that needed her so very much.

Canaan, Vermont

May 1814

Phebe glanced out the kitchen window for perhaps the hundredth time that afternoon, eagerly awaiting Joe's arrival. He had written to her that once school adjourned he was coming directly to Canaan to see her. The weather had been fair so she did not expect him to be delayed. At noon, she had harvested the first stalks of rhubarb from the sheltered lea behind the barn. Combining it with the last of the strawberry preserves, she mixed up pie filling. She carefully followed her grandmother's pie crust recipe and artfully finished off the top crust. The pie sat ready to go into the oven as soon as she heard the carriage wheels bringing her dear friend. She knew a warm pie would bring a smile to Joe's face. He was such an admirer of pie, like so many men.

She dashed up to the bedroom to change her dress, choosing a pink flowered muslin that showed little wear. It was one of only two dresses left that did not show signs of the poverty that stalked her family. She smoothed back her hair, making sure she was neat and presentable. While she had time, she pulled out Joe's last letter and read the tenderness of his words with moist eyes. Brushing away a happy tear, she tucked the letter carefully back into her workbasket. She nearly skipped down the stairs, so excited was she at the coming visit. She wondered if this was the time when Joe would finally speak his heart fully and ask her to be his wife. She knew he had college ahead of him, and they would need to wait, but she longed to have the matter settled so she could begin to make plans.

When she returned to the kitchen, the children were returning from school, clattering in with laughter and confusion, dropping books, sweaters, and lunch pails. "Is Joe here yet?" demanded Samuel.

"Not yet," replied Phebe, "I expect him anytime. In fact, I think I'll put the pie in the oven now so it's the first thing he'll smell when he walks through the door!"

Mrs. Beach arrived home just as the pie was going into the oven. "You've been busy, daughter," she said.

"Yes, Mama, I hope it's okay that I used the last of the preserves for my pie."

"Of course, my dear," her mother replied. "I'm sure Joseph will appreciate a fine piece of pie after dinner tonight."

Phebe got the children started on their homework and began dinner preparations with her mother. They chatted companionably while peeling potatoes and carrots for stew. All while they worked, Phebe kept glancing out the window for the sight of a carriage.

"He'll be along soon, I'm sure," said her mother sympathetically. "It always has been the lot of woman to wait for her man to come home." A shadow crossed her face as she remembered the one who would no longer come home. Phebe placed her arm around her mother's shoulder and gave her a comforting squeeze. The two women worked on in silence, both lost in their own thoughts.

When the pie was baked, Phebe pulled it from the oven and sat it on the counter to cool. The boys all looked up from their homework, sniffing like hungry dogs. Tommy said, "Smells good. Are we eating soon?"

"Soon enough," said his mother with a smile. Phebe glanced out the window again seeing the daylight beginning to fade a bit.

"Do you think he's been detained somewhere?" she nervously asked.

Her mother replied, "I'm sure he'll be here soon. Your young man is a man of his word. If he says he'll be here, he'll be here."

Mrs. Beach held off supper for a little longer, waiting for Joe to arrive. Finally, she said, "We may as well eat. We'll keep some stew warm for Joe when he gets here."

Phebe sat down at her place and dropped her eyes to her plate. "Maybe something has happened to him. An accident," she said softly.

Her mother glanced at her and said, "Let's not borrow trouble, little one." Turning to the rest of her brood she asked, "Whose turn is it to say grace?"

When the meal was done, the girls cleared the table. Mrs. Beach looked at Phebe and asked, "Is there dessert tonight?" Phebe was torn between wanting to save the pie for Joe and sharing it with her family.

"We may as well eat it while it's still warm," she said. Her brothers gave a shout of joy. Phebe went to the counter and picked up the knife. As she cut into the pie, a tear rolled down her cheek, dripping down onto the pie. She held one piece back in case Joe came later and split the rest up for her mother and brothers and sisters.

"Aren't you having any?" her brother Israel asked.

"No, dear," she replied. "I'm full from dinner."

After dinner, the family gathered in the parlor. While the children played marbles, Phebe read to them from Southey's The Life of Nelson, with Samuel acting out the adventures of his hero much to the amusement of the children. Bedtime came, and still Joe had not appeared. Phebe's face had taken on a drawn, worried look. Once she and her mother had the children tucked in, Phebe went to bed disheartened. When her sisters were asleep, she let go her tears of disappointment and quietly cried into her pillow.

Two weeks passed and the days grew warmer and longer. Phebe still received no word from Joe. She despaired of ever hearing from him. Unsure of the cause of his absence, she alternated between fear for his well-being and hurt and anger for his lack of correspondence. Not knowing where he was, she did not know where to send a letter. And if she had known, she was unsure what she would write to him. She was too well-mannered to voice her displeasure and too kind to take him to task for being careless of her feelings. Her mother tried to comfort her by saying all would come right in the end, but Phebe had lost her certainty in Joe's love for her.

Mrs. Beach, seeking to bring Phebe out of her sad mood, asked her to go to a neighboring farm to borrow a dozen eggs from Mrs. Blake. Phebe put on her bonnet and picked up a basket and headed out on her errand. As she walked along, she heard the sound of a carriage behind her. Glancing over her shoulder, she saw Mrs. Blake's son, Simon, riding along. Young Esquire Blake was driving a spirited horse, high stepping and tossing its mane as the carriage rolled along. He slowed the horse when he saw Phebe. Stopping, he called out to her, "Miss Beach, where are you bound on this fine morn?"

"I'm bound for your good mother's house to fetch some eggs. Our hens are not laying enough to feed all my brothers and sisters," she answered.

"Well, you're in luck," he told her, "I'm bound for the same destination, and I'd be honored to give you a ride."

Phebe demurred, "Oh, no need, sir. It's not far, and it's a fine day."

"I insist," replied the young man as he stepped down to help her into his carriage. They trotted along, exchanging pleasantries. He asked her how her family was faring since the loss of her dear father. She answered politely with little detail, not wanting to expose the precarious financial difficulties of her family to a man she knew only slightly. He glanced over at her and saw how her chin quivered a bit and her face was drawn. He pulled the carriage to the side of the road and turned to address her.

"Miss Beach, you will find I am accustomed to the troubles of others. You do not need to hide the details from me. I assure you, I am your friend, and you may rely upon me."

Phebe looked into his eyes and found honor and sincerity there. She replied, "Thank you, Mr. Blake; I do appreciate your concern for my family. It has been a very hard time for us all, especially my dear mother. We are trying to get by as best we can. It is difficult to make ends meet."

Esquire Blake nodded sympathetically and said, "Is there any way in which I can help you?"

"Perhaps there is," Phebe replied. "I am in need of work. We must have some money coming in soon. The funds I earned from teaching have run out, and I have not procured another school as yet. Perhaps you might know of one that is available? Or if I cannot find a school, perhaps I might go out to service in some respectable household."

Simon Blake stroked his chin thoughtfully. "I will make inquiries at my office and see if I can help find you a position."

"Thank you for your kindness, sir." Phebe replied.

"It is an honor for me to be of assistance to you, Ma'am." Blake spoke gently to his horse, and they continued on their way. As they rode along, the young Esquire talked of a recent trip he had taken to Concord, New Hampshire for business and told Phebe of the progress of that town and its inhabitants. Phebe found herself relaxing in his presence and in the short time it took to arrive at his mother's house, Phebe knew she had found a new friend in this fine, young man.

Canaan, Vermont

Late May 1814

At last, the ground had firmed up enough for the Beach family to begin planting the ample garden that would keep the family from want over the next year. Phebe and young Sam were swinging their hoes in the spring sunshine while the younger children planted seeds or fetched water. It was hot, muddy work, and the young people stopped often for a drink of cold well water or to rest on the garden fence. Phebe's kerchief was askew and her face and hands were covered with drying mud. She glanced up as a carriage slowed in front of the house. Automatically reaching up to tidy her hair, she realized she had just spread mud into it.

Esquire Blake leaped nimbly down from the carriage, tossing the reins over the garden fence. When he saw the disheveled state of Phebe's dress and face, he began to smile. "Well, Miss Beach, what a pleasure to see you again. You are looking quite fine today."

Phebe blushed. She glanced down at her muddy dress and back to Simon Blake's face. Making the best of it, she said, "Why, Mr. Blake, I wore my best frock in case company should come calling." Simon laughed, and Phebe gave him a twinkling smile. "What brings you by?" she asked.

He replied, "I have done as promised and made inquiries regarding a suitable position for you. I am happy to report that the dame school in Limington is in need of a school marm for the current term. The school marm who was to fill the position has decided to marry in June. The position is yours if you desire it."

Phebe's face lit up with pleasure. "I shall be honored to take the position. I must speak with mother first to see if she can spare me, but I do not think it will be a problem. Many thanks to you, sir. The income will help my family so very much. And I do so love to teach!"

Mr. Blake said quietly, "I am happy you are pleased. Now, I must speak to you about another matter, if I might do so confidentially."

"Of course," Phebe replied. She leaned her hoe against the garden fence and walked out through the gate. The good esquire leaned closer and said to her, "I am wondering, Miss Beach, if you would like to go out riding with me this evening?"

Phebe looked at him in surprise. She had not expected such an invitation. She briefly thought of Joe and how she had not heard from him. She responded, "I am honored you have asked me, but I do not know if I should. I think I have an understanding with a young man, although I am not sure of that now."

Simon Blake looked into her eyes and saw her hurt and confusion. "I never would ask you to do anything that would make you uncomfortable or stain your honor. I did not know of your arrangement. I hope you can forgive my unintentional lack of manners."

"Oh, of course, there is no need for you to apologize. I no longer know where my intended's heart and mind lie. I was to see him earlier this month, but he did not come, and I have had no letter from him. Until I know he is well, and he speaks his mind, I feel I cannot ride out with another man."

Blake nodded his head, saying, "It is what I would expect from a fine woman like you, Miss Beach. Please accept my apologies and let no awkwardness exist between us. I am your good friend, and you are mine." With that, he bade goodbye to Phebe and her siblings and, climbing into his carriage, he tipped his hat and drove away.

The Beach children continued digging and planting, lightly bantering and teasing each other as they worked. Samuel teased Phebe about her new beau, and she playfully threw a dipper of water in his direction. "Mind your tongue, whippersnapper," she warned. "I have seen the way you make cow eyes at Becky Cole!"

Phebe's mother came down the street at that moment, and Phebe ran to tell her the good news about her new teaching position. Taking her mother's market basket, the two walked together with heads close. Their talk immediately turned to making preparations for Phebe to leave for the nearby town as quickly as possible. "We must turn the hem and cuffs on your brown muslin to make them do for another school term, and we must make over my straw bonnet for you. I won't have you looking like a poor relation in front of strangers," spoke Mrs. Beach. "How troubled your father would be to see his beautiful girls going about with your clothes in such a state. The poor man worked so hard to keep you well-dressed and presentable. But how proud he would be of you, Phebe. You are a credit to him and to me, too." Tears rose in her eyes, and Phebe placed her arm around her mother's shoulders. "Dear girl, you are a blessing to me," said her mother, and the two walked arm in arm into the house.

That night after supper, Mrs. Beach directed Phebe, Martha, and Mary in the sewing projects needed to prepare Phebe's wardrobe. They worked in quiet harmony by the light of the lamps while the younger children played at their feet like a pack of squirming puppies. Mrs. Beach looked around at her fine brood of children with pride. By habit, she looked to her husband's chair to share with him that look of pride and love. She was stabbed again by the pain of missing her companion and lover and did her best to hide the tears that welled up so easily in these difficult days.

Phebe's new teaching position brought much-needed funds to her family and gave her an opportunity to put Joe Fessenden out of her mind. She still had not heard a word from him. Her new friend Esquire Blake had squired her to the home of a friend of his family, a kind widow woman who offered Phebe free room and board in exchange for help with the housework. Phebe's new school proceeded along quite well, with the children adjusting quickly to the change of teacher. As the term progressed, so, too, did Phebe's friendship with Simon Blake. He called once a week, sitting in the parlor with Phebe and Mrs. Masters, entertaining them with tales of his travels about the countryside in pursuit of his legal duties. He brought them all the news he thought might cheer them or make them laugh. Each week, the two women looked forward to his visits and for days after he left would talk about his stories.

After a month or so of his regular visits, Simon once again asked to speak with Phebe. He said, "I trust you have still not heard from your young man?"

Phebe ducked her head. "No," she said in a quiet voice, "Not a word."

"You deserve better treatment than that, Miss Beach."

She nodded in agreement and said, "I do not know what to think. He does not strike me as a man of light affections."

Simon replied, "If you so desire to write to him, I will see that the letter finds him."

Phebe looked up into Simon's sincere face and told him, "I would consider it a great kindness, Sir. I shall write it this week and have it ready for your next visit. I do thank you for your thoughtfulness!"

With the busy school week, Phebe did not have the time or energy to write the letter for several days. With Mr. Blake's visit expected on Saturday, she sat down at her desk on Friday evening after all the chores were done. Staring at a blank sheet of paper, she did not know what to write. Had Joseph spurned her affections to pursue another romantic interest? Was he sick and unable to write? Had some great tragedy befallen him, and no one knew to contact her? She did not know if her letter should chastise him for his neglect or offer sympathy for some unknown misfortune.

Dipping her pen into the inkwell, she thought of what advice her father might give her. She began to write, "Dear Mr.

Fessenden, I am at a loss for words tonight. I had expected to see you last month when school let out." The letter was brief and formal, lacking the intimacy of a letter between friends. When she was done with her inquiry, she sealed the letter in readiness for Mr. Blake. Lying down on her bed, Phebe lay with her eyes staring into the darkness, wondering what the future held for her. The moon came up, full and shining down upon her bed. Finally, just as dawn broke, she fell asleep, her path still obscured.

On Saturday, the good Esquire took her letter, promising to do all within his power to see the letter delivered. He sent it first to Joseph's family in Fryeburg with instructions for the letter to be forwarded to wherever Joseph might be. That night, Phebe wrote a letter to her mother in Canaan telling her she thought she never would marry Joseph now. It seemed as though he had forgotten her and his promises.

School continued on and when the end of the term came, Phebe prepared to return to Canaan. She had received no letters at all from Joseph, and she felt sure the tie was permanently broken. Esquire Blake offered to see her home safely, and she gladly accepted his invitation. He pressed her gently on the ride as to her feelings for Joseph. She squared her slender shoulders and admitted aloud for the first time that she thought their tie was truly broken. Simon looked at her with compassion and said, "I am truly sorry for your loss. But, in honesty, I am not disappointed for my own selfish reasons." He glanced at her to see her reaction. Her cheeks blushed a lovely shade of rose pink, and she lowered her head. "I'm so sorry, Miss Beach, I did not mean to make you uncomfortable!"

"It's not that I am uncomfortable," she replied, "I am pleased to hear you still hold me in some favor! I fear I have been a fool where Mr. Fessenden is concerned." They rode along in companionable silence for the remainder of the trip, each of them aware of the other and the possibilities that existed between them.

Arriving at the Beach home, Simon stepped down from the carriage. He reached for her hand and helped her step down. Still holding her gloved hand in his, he bowed low over it and with great courtesy said, "Miss Beach, may I have your permission to pay a formal call upon you and your family?" She acquiesced and suggested the coming Monday evening after dinner time. With a broad smile upon his face, Simon sprang into the carriage and gave Phebe a friendly wave as he drove off.

On Monday morning, Phebe made a lemon custard pie for dessert intending to serve it to Simon. She pulled it from the oven and sat it on the counter to cool. She heard a carriage pull up out front, followed by a tentative knock on the door. Opening the door, she was surprised to see the long lost Joseph Fessenden standing on the doorstep with his hat held in his hands. He looked at her nervously, not knowing what her reaction to seeing him would be. She, in turn, stared back at him not knowing what to say to his sudden appearance after months of silence.

Her mother came into the kitchen to see who was at the door. Seeing Phebe and Joseph staring wordlessly at each other, she put a cheery smile on her face saying, "Well, Mr. Fessenden, this is a surprise! Please do come in, come in. You'll want a cup of tea after your journey." Phebe stepped back and busied herself putting on the kettle. Mrs. Beach bustled about taking Joseph's coat and hat and seating him at the kitchen table as though he were a long lost family member. "And I see Phebe has just taken a pie from the oven. You arrived just in time for a good warm slice of it."

Phebe looked at her mother with dismay. The pie was not meant for Joseph. But manners dictated hospitality, so she took a plate from the cupboard and cut him a generous helping. His presence after such a long absence made her uncomfortable and fidgety. Her mother, reading the situation, said, "Well, you two must have some catching up to do. I've got to turn out the upstairs rooms today, so I'll leave you to it." Her departure left an uncomfortable silence behind.

Not knowing what to say to Joseph, Phebe sat quietly with her hands in her lap, studying the floral pattern on her tea cup. Joseph cleared his throat once and started to speak but then stopped. He tried again. "Miss Beach," he began formally. "I do not feel I deserve to call you by your familiar name. My absence has caused you to doubt my regard for you. Although that has never changed, I know I have wronged you with my silence. When I got your letter, I felt the only proper way to proceed was to come to see you. My friend, I have been working very hard to finish up at the Academy so that I can begin college as soon as I may. I do not offer that as an excuse, only as an explanation for my lack of correspondence. I began several letters to you but never finished them, always thinking I would find the time. Then time passed, and I felt as though you would be annoyed with me. I could not face that, so I again did not write. I fear I have destroyed your regard for me by my neglect." He stopped. He searched her face trying to read from her expression how she felt about him now. "Won't you talk to me, Phebe? Am I still your Joe? Are we still friends? I must know!"

The anguished look on his face stirred Phebe's warm heart. "Oh Joseph! Why did you not come in May? I so longed to see you!" Tears welled up in her eyes. "I waited for you! I thought some terrible fate had befallen you. I baked you a pie!" With that, the tears spilled over, and she put her head down on the well-worn table and sobbed.

Joseph immediately jumped from his chair and flung himself to his knees next to her. "Oh, dear girl, please don't. I can't bear to think I have been the cause of more hurt coming to you. My heart will break with it!"

Looking up, Phebe could see that his anguish matched her own. Patting his back like she would one of her young brothers, she choked out, "Let us have no more tears. Let us be friends again as we were!" With that, the two began to find their way together again. Friends must weave their lives together with care if they are to build a strong bond. Phebe and Joe spent the afternoon sitting beneath an apple tree talking about the every day happenings in their lives since last they had met.

Joe joined the Beach family for dinner, surrounded by the boisterous chattering of Phebe's brothers and sisters. When dinner was finished and the kitchen put to rights, a knock came at the door. Samuel ran to answer the door, and there stood Esquire Blake. Sam invited him into the parlor where the family was gathered. Phebe stared up guiltily, remembering that Simon had been invited to call. She stood between the two men, not sure how to proceed. Mrs. Beach introduced the two men. Simon, seeing how the wind blew, graciously recalled another engagement and politely excused himself.

Joe's brow furrowed as Simon left. He glanced at Phebe with a worried look. Was Phebe's heart warmed toward this man? Had he destroyed his chances of making her his lifetime companion? Addressing Mrs. Beach, he cordially asked her if he might take her daughter for a short stroll. Mrs. Beach nodded her agreement saying, "If Phebe wishes it."

Joe looked toward Phebe who nodded her head. The two left the house, walking down the dirt road, keeping an appropriate amount of distance between them. They walked along in silence until Joseph finally began to speak. "My darling girl," he began, turning to face her as they stood near an old elm tree, "I know I have not behaved toward you as we both would have liked me to behave. Still, I feel I must finally speak to you of my feelings and my intentions. I have told you I am bound for college and cannot marry until I have a profession to support a wife and family. But I cannot keep my silence any longer. Dropping to one knee in the twilight of the evening, he took her hand and in a husky voice, he said, "My dear girl, my friend, will you pledge your life to mine? Will you bring me joy by agreeing to be my wife?"

Phebe looked down at his dear face and saw the love in his eyes. Tempted to say yes, she thought of her father and what he would want her to do. Joe was a good man, but he was young. His regard seemed steady, but his neglect of her the past few months made her feel it was important to take her time. She responded carefully, "Dear Joe, I have such a fond regard for you, but I am not ready to give you my answer. I do not know what to do, and I feel I must talk to my mother and pray for guidance. I cannot give you my answer today."

Joe looked up at her with surprise written across his face. "I understand your hesitancy. I will make it my solemn duty to convince you of my love for you. May I expect an answer soon?"

Phebe looked down at him, "It's too soon for me to say when I shall know. It is now August. I will tell you by December. And Joe, I do not want to be pressured about this. I must be free to make up my mind. I do not want you to write to me during that time, and I will not write to you. It is the only way I will know if my heart is truly yours."

Joe Fessenden in Fryeburg, ME to Phebe Beach in Canaan, VT

November 22, 1814

My very dear Friend,

Before I leave this town where I have been since the 14th ultimo, I feel that I must write you a letter. How it will be received I cannot tell, for it will, no doubt, be unexpected as it was your request when we parted last that I should not write but wait 'til December when I should have your final answer. I will offer my excuse for disobeying you or going counter to your wish and hope and think I shall be forgiven. It is this: when the time arrives, by you proposed, to let me hear from you, you may not know in what section of the Country I am and will not write me. I shall be in New Gloucester, Maine in a few days and remain there the winter coming. Any communication, from you, by mail, will safely reach me.

May I hope you will not keep me much longer in suspense? May I hope you will, speedily after the reception of this, let me know my destiny—know whether I am to be happy in the expectation of one day calling you mine or wretched in the thought that I must leave you forever. If, my friend, the letter must be my last, be good enough to inform me what I have done to forfeit your friendship, for I am not conscious of offending in thought, word, or deed. Should the former be my happy case (which to think of perhaps is the height of presumption as I am told you said in a letter to your mother, "I shall never marry J,"), hasten to let me know it. I beg of you that I may no longer be racked by doubt, which to me is the worst of tortures. If I once possessed your affections and by my folly have forfeited those affections, think it was not intentional and pardon me. If I have been the cause of one tear falling from your eye—if I have been the cause of the heaving of one sigh from your bosom, know that I would sooner have died than cause it, and forgive me. I will say no more upon this subject.

Remember me kindly to your friends, if you please, and accept my earnest wishes for your prosperity and happiness.

Your sincere friend,

Joe P. Fessenden

P.S. Burn this letter.

P.P.S. Write me and delay not, I beg of you.

Canaan, Vermont

December 1814

The first snowfall drifted lazily down onto the streets and fields of Canaan, Vermont. Taking a moment from the busyness of the day, Phebe sat down to write the most important letter she had ever written. It was time for her to tell Joseph of her decision. "My dear friend," she began. She poured her heart out onto the page, professing the depths of her feelings for him, and giving him the answer he had waited so long to hear. Sealing the letter, she walked through the gentle snowfall to the post office, dreaming the dreams of young lovers. Handing the letter to the postmaster with a smile and exchanging a pleasantry, she went on her way, secure in the knowledge that her future was unfolding well. She felt her spirits lift as she thought of that letter winging its way to her dear friend, imagining the joy that would light up his eyes when he broke the seal and learned his fate.

New Gloucester, Maine

February 1815

Joe Fessenden returned from the post office empty-handed once again. Phebe had promised to give him her answer in December. Surely her letter would have reached New Gloucester by now. Stamping his boots to remove the snow, he pulled off his hat and gloves and hung his coat on the peg by the door. He walked into his brother Samuel's study and slumped down in a chair. Sam looked up from a brief he was writing. "No letter, again?" Joe shook his head, sunk in gloom. Sam sat looking at his young brother, wondering what to do or say to make him feel better. Screwing up his courage, he said, "Don't you think it's time you wrote to her?"

Joe glanced up and said, "She told me not to write. She said she'd write to me. She said she'd give me her answer in December. I can only think she means to spurn me in favor of Esquire Blake. Women are fickle creatures!" With that, Joe flung himself out of his chair and left the room.

Sam's wife entered the room, just as Joe, looking as cheerful as sleet in May, left it. "Still no letter?" she asked Sam.

"No, and he's giving up hope."

"I'm surprised at Phebe," said Deborah, "She doesn't strike me as a girl who would trifle with the affections of a young man. I do hope no more harm has come to her family."

"All I know," replied Sam, "Is that my brother is getting more and more impossible to live with."

Deborah got a thoughtful look on her face. "I may have an idea that could help." She dropped a kiss on the top of Sam's head, and headed out of the study.

At dinner a few nights later, Deborah announced her sister, Elizabeth, was coming on a visit for a few weeks. Sam looked knowingly in her direction, but she ignored his glance.

Joe Fessenden in New Gloucester, Maine to Phebe Beach in Limington, VT

July 7, 1815

My good Friend,

I received with the greatest pleasure a few lines from you this morning—I am indeed grateful for I had supposed myself entirely forgotten or remembered only with contempt. They are the first and all I have had the happiness to receive since we parted more than a year ago. I wrote you last November from Fryeburg reminding you that the time was close at hand when, according to promise, you were to inform me whether I might continue my connection or not, and told you I was about going to New Gloucester to reside a few months with my brother where any communication would reach me per mail.

Your "long letter", my friend, you say you have written me has never arrived. You can judge (though no fault of yours) that it was not without cause I thought you had forgotten me—nay, worse—considered me beneath the notice of a farewell line. I regret extremely your letter did not reach me, and why it did not I cannot imagine. It must, I think, be owing to the stupidity or knavery of some of the Postmasters.

I have some reason to believe from the complexion of the letter I just received that you have still some friendship for me, and would to God I had known it sooner, then should I not have passed so many gloomy hours. Then I had not so long have been tormented by the cutting and bitter thoughts that she, whose esteem was almost my only hope of happiness in this world, had forsaken me without assigning a reason why. It was indeed unfortunate for my peace for the last ten months and has given you some cause to suspect that I was inconstant, but surely I have not been in fault. How did you send your letter is an inquiry I will here make?

I have taken my pen a number of times within the last five months to write you, but I as often remembered that I had already gone counter to your request in writing my last letter, and I remembered, too, our conversation when I was at your Mother's last, and my proud spirit would not let me further beg your love. You perceive that I have had good grounds to think that if you ever had anything like friendship for me it was done away. And you have had some grounds to suppose the same of me, merely by the miscarriage of a letter. Worried have been my feelings at times, in consequence of your supposed neglect, or other reason. At times, I almost waged war against the whole female sex. Thinking myself coquetted by one, I have considered them unstable and ingenuous, vapourous and evanescent as the fog of the morning.

Yes, and frequently when I have been with them, I have said in my heart, "Insects! Away—ye flies of fashion ye! Fluttering nothing." This was, to be sure, wrong, but it was natural. My heart melted when I saw your name this morning, and I found my whole soul was with you. But enough of this, I will go to your letter. You wish to know "what was my determination?" I tell you without reserve for you know I always have dealt openly and sincerely with you, I am, as I ever have been, wholly yours. My affection for you has not altered in the least. If you cannot love me well enough to marry me, I shall as soon as I get my degree at college go to the city of New York and study law. If you can, I shall as soon as I get out of college settle down in some business and will marry you. I shall, God willing, get through in two years.

I have disposed of my farm and have my little fortune in ready money so that I can go anywhere I please and carry my all. I am willing to consult your happiness in every thing. If you consider yourself under obligations to marry me and think you cannot get off without violating a promise and wish to get off, I will release you at once from all obligation. If, on the contrary, you do love me and would like to marry me, my best endeavours ever shall be to make you happy. Consult your own feeling in all things and whether I am to have the happiness of marrying you or not, I will always be your friend in truth.

I hope you will write me immediately about this and tell me everything—what are your circumstances, how are you engaged, what is most necessary to promote your happiness in this world? What are your feelings toward me? Do write me soon and direct your letter to this town. Send it in one to your Uncle or Aunt and let it be put into the mail at Fryeburg lest like the other it should not reach me. I repeat, I am wholly yours—I am not changed in the least. Whatever will most promote your happiness will most promote mine. I repeat, do write me and be explicit. You cannot mistake me. You know what are my feelings toward you. If you think you can love me well enough to marry me, tell me so, and if it is agreeable, I will visit you next September or January, the times of college vacations. If you tell me no, I will ever say God bless you and ever be your sincere friend.

Joe P. Fessenden

Canaan, Vermont

July 15, 1815

Phebe's sunny smile told her mother everything she needed to know. After so long of not hearing from Joe, Phebe's spirits had been sunk quite low. With the coming of Joe's long overdue letter, Phebe had a lightness to her step that Polly had not seen since before that dark day when all their lives had changed. Perhaps some good could still come for them all. Phebe bustled through her morning chores so she could reply to Joe's letter.

Sitting at the kitchen table with the late morning sun shining warm upon her back, the copper highlights in her hair shining like a new penny, Phebe poured her heart out to Joe after the long months of worrying and wondering. Finishing the letter, she took it immediately to the post office. Handing it to the postmaster, she received another letter back to her from her Aunt Abigail in Fryeburg. Phebe returned home, outwardly sedate and proper, but inwardly gamboling like a spring lamb. Her Joe loved her still.

Arriving home, Phebe opened her aunt's letter and began to read. The contents of the letter stunned her. She dropped into a chair in the kitchen, staring straight ahead, shocked. Could this be true? Her dear aunt would surely not make something like this up. Joe—her Joe—keeping company with another woman? It had to be a mistake. After all his protestations of love for her? Could it be true? If it was, how could she ever believe a word he said? Aunt Abigail reported the woman was his brother Samuel's sister-in-law, and it was "well known" in Fryeburg that he was spending much time with her.

Polly Beach entered the kitchen to find her daughter with her head on the kitchen table, weeping. Kneeling beside her, she asked, "What has happened? Phebe, do tell me!"

Phebe threw herself into her mother's arms, weeping. "Aunt Abigail says Joe has betrayed me with another woman. I shall never marry him now."

Her mother held Phebe out from her so she could see her face. "Can this be true?"

Phebe handed the letter to her mother. "See for yourself!"

Polly quickly read the letter. "You must write to Joseph immediately and demand he give you some explanation of this!"

Phebe wiped tears from her face. "I am not sure I can write that letter, Mother. It is all too embarrassing. How could he? How could he?"

Phebe went to her room and read Joe's letter again. Then, she read Aunt Abigail's letter again. Folding both letters closed, she picked up her pen and began to write.

From Joseph Fessenden in Fryeburg to Phebe Beach in Limington, VT

Feb. 22, 1816

My Dear Friend,

Doubtless, you have thought it strange that I have not answered your kind letter, which was duly and timely received long ere this, and still stranger that I have not, agreeable to my promise, made you a visit. I will tell you how it has happened that I have done neither and am confident I shall be acquitted of what might otherwise be considered ungentlemanly neglect. I did not receive your letter 'til college term was so far gone that I thought a line from me would not reach you before vacation commenced, when I should see you and whisper in your own ear how warm with affection my heart beats toward you and how grateful I was for your frankness in saying "your heart was at my service" —a declaration so necessary to my peace and happiness.

But when the time arrived, and I was on the tip-toe of anticipation of again clasping your hand, a school was offered me and at such high wages that my friends thought it would be wrong in me not to take it, that I could write you everything necessary to be said, and that for $50 for eight weeks I ought to change my visit 'til the next vacation which would take place 3rd Wednesday of May next. I accordingly engaged myself and wrote you a long letter, which I enclosed in one to a friend of mine in this town, with directions to send it by private conveyance if any such could be found, and if not, to send it per mail in a wrapper subscribed to your Grandpa as I had reason to believe some gentleman has had the politeness to stop some letters from each of us. That man lives in Lancaster. You will know whom I mean.

By some fatality, which forever attends me, this letter did not reach this town, and I was ignorant of it 'til within a fortnight. My dear girl, you must know this. Since the summer of 1813, my affections have been entirely with you and no other! I am grieved that you must once again leave home to earn your sustenance. I would that you had not to do that. I have enough money to keep you from hardship, and I want only to shield you from insult. If only I could be with you and tell you all of this in person!

Never for an instant believe these rumours to be based on any truth. If you honour the heart of Joseph P. Fessenden, you certainly would be far from harbouring even a suspicion of his being such a "scoundrel."

Yours in sincerity,

JP Fessenden

After reading the letter, Phebe folded it and taking her pen, she wrote on the flap of the letter:

Tis the last time, tis the last!!

I will not, I cannot believe the man who wrote this is such a villain as report affirms. It is not possible!!

"Did you honour the heart of JPF you certainly would be far from harbouring even a suspicion of his being such a 'scoundrel.'"

I will not believe it yet.

Canaan, Vermont

Late May 1816

All through the month of May, Phebe waited to hear from Joe. She barely dared to raise her hopes that he would appear as planned. She'd had no letter from him in many weeks. It seemed he would always be disappointing her. She could not understand his silence and his absence. Where once she would have made excuses or given him the benefit of the doubt, or even worse, worried herself sick over his health and safety, now she doubted his regard. Her mother told her some men behaved such that a woman could never be sure of their feelings.

Joe seemed such a good man, steady in his regard. But then again, he would fall silent and fail to keep his promises. Which man was the real Joseph Fessenden? Phebe often tossed and turned at night, beset by worries about her family's precarious financial situation, and by her sad confusion over Joe's actions. Did he love her as he said? Or was what her aunt told her really true. Was Joe courting another? If he was, then that meant he could not be trusted in anything he said or did. Or was she wronging a good and decent man by believing idle gossip about him? If that was the case, then it was she who was at fault—she who was wronging him.

Canaan, Vermont

Late July 1816

After several weeks of waiting and wondering and torturing herself with thoughts that went round and round in her head, she at last put her head down in her dear mother's lap and sobbed out her hurts. Polly Beach's heart broke to see her daughter in such pain. Wrapping herself around Phebe, she whispered soothing words, holding the girl until her tears slowed. Phebe looked up at her with red, swollen eyes and the tears still drying on her face, "What am I to do, Mother! What am I to do?" Polly brushed back the hair from Phebe's face, desperately wanting to make the hurt stop and not knowing how. Taking a deep breath, she gently said, "Phebe, any man who does not treasure you and cherish you is a fool. And I would not have my daughter marry a fool. Your dear father would not want you to marry someone not worthy of you. You must do as you think best, but perhaps it is time for you to ask Joseph to release you from your connection. It may well be that God has a different man in mind for you."

Phebe looked lovingly at her mother. She ever did want what was best for her children. As much as Phebe wanted to believe that Joe was the man she would spend her life with, perhaps her mother was right. She would write once more to Joe. If he did not respond quickly, she would know it was time to close the door to the future she so longed for with him. Taking her pen in hand, she once again poured out her heart to the man who had so often called her his dear friend. When the letter was done, her spirit was lighter as she walked in the July sunshine to the post office. She would leave this in God's good hands.

On the way back from the post office, Simon Blake came riding down the main street on a fine looking, spirited mare. He pulled up the horse when he saw her. Dismounting gracefully, he stepped up to Phebe with a warm smile on his face. Bowing over her hand, he cheerfully said, "My dear Miss Beach, what a pleasant vision you are to me on such a fine day."

Phebe smiled in return saying, "Dear Squire Blake, have we not been friends long enough now so that we might be Phebe and Simon to one another?"

Simon looked surprised at Phebe's request and immediately agreed. Pressing his advantage, he asked respectfully, "Phebe, might I call upon you this evening? Perhaps we might take a carriage ride, the weather is so fine." Phebe readily agreed and the two parted ways with light hearts.

September 24, 1816 Joseph Fessenden in Fryeburg to Phebe Beach in Canaan

My dear Friend,

I received your truly kind and affectionate letter, dated July 29 about five weeks since, in which you very properly ask an explanation of my conduct, breach of promise, long silence, etc. In truth, my dear girl, I hardly know what to say. Suspicion is undoubtedly strong against me, and should I give reasons, which might appear rational to unprejudiced minds and undoubtedly to yours, did not uncharitable people interfere and persuade, my enemies and your friends will say it is deception all together, and longer to believe the liar would be the height of folly and madness. I make these observations, because you know and I know that one of your relations in this place is apt to be uncharitable toward me. But I have ever dealt plainly and honestly with you Phebe, and ever will continue so to do, whatever may be the event.

It is true I did say if I live I will see you next May. The expression was too strange, but such was my determination at the time. What then, you ask, induced me to alter that determination? I answer. It had been confidently told me that you had received the attentions of our truly noble friend S.A.B. Esquire. This, I was disposed to believe 'til it was too late to fulfill my engagement. I believed this report, because there were formerly some mysterious circumstances attending your treatment of me, which, I could interpret no other way than that you had some other object more worthy of your regard, which you had thought of possessing. These circumstances, and your wish to dissolve our connection without assigning any reasons why or wherefore, and your repeated declarations to me by letter that you were most unhappy and never should be happier led me to believe this. This object I thought was the Esquire and that the reason of your writing me as you did the summer before last was because you were mistaken in obtaining this object and would consent on the whole to take me "Jack at a pinch" to use a vulgar proverb.

When I was informed that the Esquire had actually made you a visit, I concluded you would again wish to be released from me and that it was best to stay where I was—bow in silence and wait the event. I now find it was all together an error—that it was ever jealousy and folly in me thus to have believed that the Esquire was directed as he always is, by truly benevolent motives and those only. Such was my explanation; such were my reasons and perhaps natural enough for a person as fond as I am. I resolved after receiving your last letter to see you this vacation. But at the close of the college term, I found that pestilence had made such a sad sweep among my friends in New Gloucester and continued its ravages so long that time could hardly be spared to let me leave this place. My brother has been sick, his wife dangerously so—her father's family, who

69

have always treated me with kindness, most sadly afflicted, the mother and one daughter (to whom it has been reported I was attached) dead, and all the rest save one young man on beds of sickness.

It is a reality, I believe, that emphatically there is a sad fatality continually hanging about me. I shall never say again I will visit you at any determined period but hope, God willing, to have that pleasure next January. I shall state to you now as I did in my last letter that my affections and best wishes are with you—ever have been and ever will be, I presume. Let what will happen. I thank you for saying you will not believe me a scoundrel 'til I personally or by letter tell you it is so. I believe you will never find me villainous toward you; however, I may be in other respects. I have ever told you the serious sentiments of my heart and will be as generous in future with you as you say you will be with me, never to believe any reports unfavourable 'til sanctioned by yourself. The time may come, I trust it will, when we shall walk hand in hand in pure affection, and after doing our duty in this uncertain and treacherous world through the merits of our Glorious Saviour, wing our way to a happy immortality above.

I shall never be able to say one half I want to communicate to you in this letter. I beg you will write immediately and often, as I will you. Express your feelings and views fully and without reserve as I ever have and ever shall. Continue, if you can, to cherish affection for me, and if not, let me know it as soon as possible. I will do the same with you. I hope you will put no unfavourable construction on what I have written. I can assure you it is meant for good. Your Aunt, I believe, will be always disposed to think me not honest. My brother has committed errors in his dealings with the fairer sex, therefore, she concludes I shall, too. But your views are too noble to be disturbed by her idle suspicions and distrust. Remember me kindly to all your friends. Write often, do. Direct your letters to College.

Yours sincerely and affectionately,

JP Fessenden

Phebe Beach in Canaan, VT to Joseph Fessenden at Bowdoin College, Brunswick, Maine

October 13th, 1816

Dear Friend,

I thank you for your kind letter which was timely received and gave me much satisfaction. I had about concluded I should never hear more from you after anxiously waiting through the whole of September (which I knew to be the time of vacation) without hearing or seeing anything of you. But I hope now for more ease, as you appear to be satisfied about the Esquire's courtship. He is one of the best of men, and I hope I shall ever love and respect him in the manner I ought.

As to my recounting of my troubles in my letters, the trials my family has faced were sufficient cause for my melancholy, and so I determined that I might never again be happy in this life. It gave me relief to recount my troubles to a person who appeared to be so deeply interested in my afflictions and so much concerned for my welfare as you appeared to be when I last saw you. But, as I have never had any reason to doubt your word, I shall make no further comments upon the subject. I am so accustomed to recount my afflictions that I can think of little else to write. Yet, if they cause any disagreeable apprehensions, perhaps it would be as well to forbear.

I have no news. As to my situation, it is no better, and it cannot be worse. I am with my dear mother, and I shall be until I can get a school which will be about a month. My health is good and spirits as good as my situation will permit. This news will be of little consequence to you unless you feel as anxious on my account as I do on yours. I wish you to write every opportunity and write very particularly. I am in great haste, for the one who is to carry this to Fryeburg is waiting. Please accept my best wishes and believe me ever your friend.

Sincerely,

Phebe P. Beach

Canaan, Vermont

May 1817

Sixteen-year-old Samuel Beach lay passed out cold on the stable floor. Around him, his drinking companions conducted a raucous poker game amidst clouds of cigar smoke. Alfred Cole tossed a copper into the pot saying, "I'll see that and raise it." Tossing another coin in the growing pile, he glanced down at the young man on the floor. "Boy just can't handle his rum." He nudged Sam with his foot.

Sam opened bleary, red-rimmed eyes, looking up confused. "Whaddya kick me for?" he slurred.

"Time you go home to your mama, boy," replied Henry Dennet.

"Don't you bring my mother in to this, Dennet. S'your father's fault she's a widow." Sam stumbled up awkwardly from the floor.

Dennet replied, "If your old man wasn't a traitor trading with the British, my father wouldn't a hadda shoot him, would he?" At that, Sam charged Dennet, upsetting the table as cards and coins flew into the air. Dennet shoved Sam backwards. He hit the wall, the wind knocked out of him. Alfred tried to stop Sam from charging again, but Sam shoved his friend back and lunged for Dennet again. Dennet drew back his arm and landed a solid right cut to Sam's face. Sam retaliated with a blow that glanced off Dennet's nose, causing blood to spurt onto both their shirts.

As fists flew, the young men all joined the fray, at first laughingly and then in dead seriousness, giving vent to the aggressions long buried by polite society. The older men grew tired of the fracas and spilled out into the street, heading for home to bind their wounds and sleep off their dissipation. Wrapping their arms around each other, they walked down the main street of Canaan singing in rum-soaked tones.

In the stable, Alfred Cole leaned down to help Sam up. Sam smacked away the proffered hand, saying, "Lea' me 'lone." Alfred shrugged and left Sam where he was, heading off to his own house. When dawn broke, Sam Beach woke and sat up groggily. His head pounding, he struggled to his feet, swaying unsteadily. Moving slowly and painfully, his head and eye throbbing, he stumbled home. Trying to open the kitchen door quietly, hoping his mother was not yet up, Sam stumbled over the doorstep and sprawled on the kitchen floor. He lay where he fell, filthy, bloodied, and reeking of tobacco smoke and rum.

At the sound of the door opening, Phebe, sitting at the kitchen table, glanced up from the letter she was writing to Joe in time to see her young brother fall. She leapt up from the table and rushed to where he lay. "Sam! Sam! What is it? What's happened?" She recoiled from the stench of him. "Oh, Sam! What have you done?" she demanded.

Sam rolled over onto his back, looking into her face, "Hello, Sister. What are you doing up there?" He gave her a sloppy grin and reached up to pat her face.

"Sam! You must get up off this floor at once. What would Mother think if she saw you right now? Hasn't she had enough trouble of late?"

Sam looked chagrined at the thought. "Okay, okay, I'll get up. I just need to close my eyes for a minute."

Phebe spoke sharply to him, "Sam! You get up off this floor this instant!" Clumsily, Sam struggled to his feet and stood swaying. Phebe looked at him with exasperation. "Oh, Sam, what is to be done with you? Come with me." Taking him by the hand she led him to the kitchen basin and began cleaning the blood from his face. He winced when she cleaned around his eye, which during the night had swollen nearly shut. He had another bruise on his chin, and his knuckles where skinned and raw. "What would father think to see what has become of his oldest son?" Phebe admonished him.

Sam ducked his head in embarrassment. "I know I do wrong, Phebe. I just can't seem to help myself," Sam said sheepishly.

In an exasperated tone Phebe said, "Go out to the pump and clean yourself up. Throw that shirt in the waste bin. It's beyond repair. And don't come back in until you're presentable. Do you want the children to see you like this?" Sam's shoulders dropped. Taking the towel Phebe handed him, he went out back to clean up.

Phebe sat down and continued her letter to Joe, filling him in on her concerns for her favorite brother. His soul was surely in danger of being lost forever if he did not curb his drinking. Without a father's firm hand, Sam had gotten himself into one scrape after another. It wasn't just the drinking, though that was bad enough. Sam had also taken to cussing, smoking, and telling pitiable stories. Phebe missed her father's wise council for herself, but even more so for Sam. She must try harder to give him the guidance he needed to become a man her father would be proud of.

Joseph Fessenden at Bowdoin College to Phebe Beach in Fryeburg

June 28ᵗʰ, 1817

My good girl,

Another week has passed, and it is with peculiar pleasure that I lay aside my books and retire to my study to write you a letter. I cannot address you with the ordinary common place feelings of friendship. I must express that warm attachment and sincere affection for you which I now feel. You were always dear to me, always beloved, but never half so much formerly as at the present time. A reason for this is easily assigned. When I, by my folly, had forfeited all right to your esteem, I thought that if I ever saw you again, I should see a repulsive, indignant frown upon your brow. To my surprise, I was met with a smile, forgiven, and restored to your confidence. Happy disappointment!

Surely you deserve a double portion of gratitude. And let me tell you, you have it—are much more closely wound round my heart than ever before. Yes, and I am persuaded I shall hold you there, 'til the vital spark which animates my body shall have flown forever. Do not think me romantic if I apply the strong expression of my favourite poet as a just representation of my feelings.

"Wert thou as far

As that vast shore washed by the farthest sea,

I would adventure for such merchandise"

With pleasure, mingled with pain, I look back to the time when we were engaged in academic duties, and enjoyed the sweets of friendship. With pleasure, because it was then I formed that acquaintance with you, which, with the blessings of Heaven, will render my journey of life pleasant and happy. With pain, because I am never to be occupied in those scenes again because I neglected the advantages and enjoyed and wasted a part of that time, which Providence, in mercy, had given me to prepare myself for usefulness in the world, and a happy immortality beyond the grave.

It is with deep regret that I reflect on my total disregard of the religious instructions with which in early life I was favoured. Alas! How much of my youth has been spent in the tents of wickedness. This retrospect of the past I frequently take and find it for my advantage. It serves as a stimulus to enable me "to redeem the time, to press forward toward the mark for the prize of the high calling." This, in fact, is the bounden duty of every person. The Christian, especially, will perceive guilt if he lets a day pass without reflecting how it has been spent. Should the sinner do this in apprehension and feelingly, as well as speculatively, realize his situation that he is slumbering on the brink of total ruin. That this is his only probationary state that as death leaves him, so will judgment find him. That each moment is calling him nearer the shores of eternity. Is adding sin upon sin to the already black and dismal catalogue, he would be roused.

Why, were there no other guide than conscience, it seems to me, its admonitions would convince anyone of cool reflection that they were but the gentler corrodings of the fire that never dies. The more moderate searchings of that fire which is never quenched. But unhappily, the sinner stifles consciousness; he will not hearken to the warning voice; he turns a deaf ear 'til that Being, who arrests the winged lightning in its course and smooths the billows of the ocean, warns him of his danger, and draws him to Himself.

My dear friend, my own transgressions have caused me to see my way to the path my life must follow. I have determined to dedicate my life to walking in the footsteps of our dear Lord and Saviour as did my father before me. I have seen how easily man falls into sinful, selfish transgressions. As such, my desire now is to guide them, reprove them, and encourage them to walk in the ways of righteousness. I would walk the path of a true Christian. Oh, my dear girl, I do not feel I can walk that path without you by my side. Could you consent to live the life of a parson's help meet? Is it too much to presume upon your affections for me that you might consent to walk beside me, sharing my difficulties?

I fear I am resigning you to a life of penury and want. I would not wish that for you. Be assured, I will ever provide for you in any way I must. Your happiness is paramount to me. I would not have you suffer one moment from lack. But, my Phebe, I do feel so strongly that God is calling me, calling us, to serve in His great mission field. Could you consent to such a plan? Please do tell me, and be explicit. I want to know all of your thoughts and feelings as to the future we will share together.

I hope a protecting Angel is hovering near you, and you are quietly asleep. Tell your Aunt I remember her with gratitude, and tell her I hope she will fight the good fight of faith and receive a never-fading crown at last. Give my regards to your Uncle, and ask him from me, seriously to examine the 23 verse of the 2 chapter of Acts. The doctrine, which I advocated and he opposed, is there fully exhibited. Give my love to Abigail and the little boys. Kiss Mary Ann for me. Your brother, Samuel, is well, is a good boy, and boards with me. It rejoiced my mother and sister very much to hear that our connection was renewed. They love you. Take good care of your health and if consistent, remain at Fryeburg until the fall and let me have the pleasure of gallanting you home. I should take it very kindly if you would write me. But consult your own feeling. I am never to solicit anything, you know, that is irksome to you. The cough with which I was afflicted when I left you has left me. My health is good. Excuse the mess of this scrawl. That Heaven may protect and bless you ever is the sincere and earnest prayer of your friend, Joe P. Fessenden

From Joseph Fessenden in Fryeburg to Widow Mary Beech in Canaan, Vermont

Sept. 16, 1817

Respected Madam,

It probably gives you pleasure at all times to hear from Phebe, and I take the liberty, through the medium of the mail, to give you information of her. Perhaps you have not heard of her recent sickness, or, if you have, are ignorant of the event of it and are tortured with all the anxiety of an affectionate mother for her welfare. I can inform you that she has been very sick with the dysentery at Concord, where she went a few weeks since, to visit her friend Miss Bradley but is now recovering. She has had a grievous and painful disorder but, by the blessing of God, is out of danger and will shortly again be restored to health. I left her a week ago in pretty good spirits. She will return to this place as soon as she is able to ride.

In her illness, every attention has been paid her. Nothing which could contribute to her comfort and restoration to health has been left undone. Wherever she is known she is universally and deservedly beloved. In Concord, not only her immediate friends, but strangers who had had but a slight acquaintance with her were particularly interested in her fate, and rendered every assistance to her in their power. Poor girl! She has been sorely afflicted in her youth. Her morning sun has emphatically been obscured by clouds, dark and gloomy, but, I trust in God, its meridian will be splendid, and its setting prosperous, honourable, and peaceful. The arm of the Almighty has been laid heavily upon her but only to fit her for another and better world.

Her permission and desire, together with my own strong inclinations, induce me to write you this letter. Some circumstances, dear madam, have occurred since I was last at your house, which have given you and your family reason to doubt the sincerity of my professions of the connection between Phebe and myself. If you have not already been apprised of it, I can tell you that all difficulties subsisting between us are now happily removed and amicably settled. Of this, I have abundant reason to be thankful and confidently hope neither she nor you will ever have cause to regret it. It will be needless to give you, in this letter, my reasons for a course of conduct which led Phebe and her friends to suspect my motives and constancy with regard to her. I hope to see you ere long and will then make an explanation. In the mean time, if she will forgive me and pardon my errors, I am persuaded you will not withhold your consent to our reconciliation.

From my first acquaintance, I have been strongly attached to your family and have wept for your unhappy afflictions. Although it has never yet been in my power to alleviate your sorrows in the past, I trust the time is not far distant when I shall both have the ability and inclination to do it and can succeed in wiping away the tears which have too long streamed from the eyes of those I love.

In all your trials and disappointments and troubles, you have had the consolations of the gospel for your support. You know that your redeemer liveth. That he who has promised to be the widow's God and husband is not like man that he should lie or do wrong but one who is constant and sure, and that, by his sacrifice, you will finally be delivered from all tribulation and advanced to the joys of an endless eternity of rest. These are glorious anticipations and are peculiar to the Christian. These enable us to meet, with unshaken fortitude, all the trials, the perplexities, and evils of this difficult, inconstant, and wicked world. If we put our trust in God and humble ourselves under a sense of our sins and aberrations from Him, we need fear nothing. The storms of life will beat upon us in vain.

You, my dear madam, though greatly afflicted, can say with the Shumanite of old when the servant of the Prophet interrogated her of her family, "all is well." To the humble believer, the promises of the gospel are consolations which the world cannot give nor take away. If we persevere and hold out to the end in a Christian course, we are sure of a reward. The great apostles could say and be happy in the reflection, notwithstanding all his labours and persecutions, "I have fought a good fight. I have kept this faith, and there is laid up for me a crown of glory which the righteous Judge will give me at that day." This crown of glory awaits every humble follower of the Lord Jesus Christ. It awaits you, I trust, and will be the happy portion of all your children.

Within the last year, my attention has been called up to the contemplations of things divine and eternal. By the good Spirit of God, I hope I have been led to see my deep depravity and guilt and, by His grace, have been led to repentance. To do the will of my Heavenly Father is now my governing object. But I find I have many things to contend with. Enemies within and without assail me. Well may the life of a Christian be compared to warfare. I find I have constant need of divine assistance to guide me in the pathways of duty. I find I must take up my cross daily and be willing to follow the Lamb of God whithersoever He bids.

I do not know but it will fatigue you to read this long letter, and I will come to a close. Religion is becoming my favourite theme, and I wish to be thinking of it and speaking of it all the time. You will pardon any thing I have said amiss. Phebe's health,

I think, after her recovery will probably be better than it has been for some time before. I hope you will be willing to let her spend the winter in Fryeburg. I am persuaded it will be both for her comfort and advantage, and if she can be of no essential service to you at home, you will be willing to forego the pleasure of her society, for her benefit. I trust the good hand of God will ever be upon you and yours. Give my love, if you please, to your children. With the most profound respect and sincere regard, I am your friend and humble servant.

Joseph P. Fessenden

Bowdoin College, Brunswick, Maine

January 1819

Joe Fessenden sat in the chapel on a sunny Sunday morning. The other Bowdoin students had already filed out. As a hush fell over the church, Joe leaned his head upon his hands as they rested on the pew in front of him. So quiet and still was he, that he might well be thought to have passed over to his heavenly reward. He'd felt a change coming over him slowly during his time at Bowdoin. A quiet certainty growing within him. A holy fire was kindling. A fire that would change the course his life would take. Knowing so much now of the ills of society and the deep depravity of men's souls, Joe felt called to work in God's mission field, to follow his minister father's path.

The certainty of this life-altering decision had grown stronger with each passing day. He meditated on the errors and sins he had committed in the course of his young life. He had seen the mistakes of others he knew and the effect those mistakes had on loved ones. He had a deep compassion for the widow, the orphan, the prisoner, the sick, and the dying. He had already seen so much sadness in the world, so much injustice, so much wrong. And so, in the quiet church, Joseph Palmer Fessenden gave his life to Jesus Christ, vowing to be His hands and His heart in a world torn by strife. With that vow, with that surrender, Joe Fessenden set his feet upon an unknown path, but a path he was certain was the only path he could walk.

Canaan, Vermont

November 1819

The day dawned gray, and the air was crisp with the promise of the long winter ahead. The Beach family arose early, anxious to begin the day. Many tasks lay still ahead—the tasks that are made simpler by the joy that accompanies them. Mrs. Beach tied her apron around her waist and set to work making breakfast for the family. Her usual partner in this endeavor had been given the day off. Martha and Mary stepped in to fill their sister's shoes, mixing the pancake batter and frying the bacon on the woodstove.

Abby mooned about underfoot, torn between the romance of a wedding and the jealousy of not being the center of attention. Mrs. Beach looked at her with gentle exasperation as Abby sighed loudly for the tenth time. "Abby," she said calmly, "Would you be a good girl and arrange the greens and the bittersweet in the china bowl. You always do it so prettily." Abby sighed again but was mollified by the balm to her ego. Samuel was out in the barn milking the cow. He'd taken Isaac and Israel with him to muck out the stalls and Tommy to collect eggs. Sergeant set the plates and silverware. All were happy, bustling, and excited for the day.

In the upstairs bedroom she'd shared for years with her sisters, Phebe was taking a last look around. This would be the last time she saw this room through the eyes of a girl. By this afternoon, she would be a married woman. Married! At last! To her dear Joseph. So many sorrows and joys all taken together had led up to this day. She thought about the misunderstandings that had nearly broken their connection. They had come so close to losing each other. She thought about Joe being so close by at her uncle's house. She was not to see him until she walked down the stairs to the parlor this afternoon.

She was by turns overjoyed and frightened. Today she was joining her life with another. Everything would change in that one moment, with that one decision. What would the future hold for her and her Joe? She had no way of knowing. But one thing she did know. She had chosen well. Joe had proven himself to be a good, steady man, a kind and thoughtful man. He cared for her, for her widowed mother, her fatherless brothers and sisters. A good man who would stand strong beside her whatever burdens and troubles might come. Shaking herself from her reverie, she smoothed her hair, pulled her dressing gown on, and headed downstairs for breakfast.

When she walked into the kitchen, the family was all gathered round the table, and they turned as one to look at her. Phebe's mother rose from her chair and holding her arms wide, pulled her eldest child close. Kissing her on the cheek, she whispered to her, "My dear girl."

Phebe melted into her mother's embrace and placed a kiss on her mother's cheek, whispering, "My dear mother."

The tender moment was broken by Samuel who demanded, "Let's not let a good breakfast get cold!" Laughing, the family joined together in the last breakfast they would ever share before this next big change to their family circle.

Once breakfast was cleared away, Mrs. Beach marshaled her troops for the final preparations. Every inch of the house must be perfect for the guests. A stream of neighbors stopped by bringing extra chairs, salads, casseroles, and small gifts for the bride and groom. At noon time, Mrs. Beach took her daughter by the hand and led her upstairs to her bedroom. She sat Phebe down on the edge of the bed and said, "I wanted to talk to you, just the two of us, before all the guests arrive." She began to tear up. "Your father and I often talked about the kind of men we would like our daughters to marry. We wanted you each to find happiness with a good man. Someone to stand by you when times were hard. But even more, we wanted each of you to find someone who made you smile, made you laugh. My child, we can never know how long we have together." She paused as a tear rolled down her cheek, lost for a moment in her own grief.

"Here is what your father and I would always have you remember. You must cherish the happiness that comes. Hold close the goodness. Never take a moment of it lightly. It is those good memories that will bind you close and be a comfort to you should life deal you more cruel blows. And that is the best advice I can give you. Always know that you have a family who loves you. That is a light that will shine brightly for you all your life." Then, reaching into her apron pocket, Polly Beach pulled out the necklace given to her by her own mother on her wedding day. Placing it around her daughter's neck, she kissed her on the cheek and said, "May the Lord guide you and keep you all the days of your life."

Phebe wiped away the tears that ran down her cheeks and, holding her mother close, she said, "You ever were the best and dearest of mothers." Rising from the bed, they stepped across the hall to the girls' bedroom where Mary, Martha, and Abby were eagerly awaiting their sisters' prerogative of dressing the bride.

Downstairs, Samuel was acting the host, ushering the guests into the parlor with the help of Israel and Isaac. Tommy and Sergeant stood outside overseeing the arrival of the guests. At ten 'til two, the nervous groom entered the parlor, twisting his hat in his hands, tugging at his collar, and smiling the most foolish smile ever smiled by a groom. Today, his pretty Phebe, his dear friend, was joining her life to his.

At the appointed hour, the Beach sisters descended the stairs one by one, each in her best Sunday dress. Then came the bride's mother, a gentle smile on her face while tears stood in her eyes. How her dear companion would have loved this day. She could feel his spirit with her. Then, at the top of the stairs with all eyes upon her stood Miss Phebe Beach. Small and fragile, aglow with love, her eyes seeing only one person in that crowded parlor. And Joe gazing up at her, his eyes holding hers. Two souls alone in a crowd. Phebe descended the stairs and took her place next to the man who would walk with her from now until the end of time. She slipped her shaking hand into his, and together they stood before their families and God and pledged their lives, one to the other.

Kennebunkport, Maine

1820

The carriage pulled to a stop in front of a small meeting house on Kennebunkport's main street. Joe Fessenden looked into his pretty wife's eyes for courage as he swung himself down from the seat. After his student preaching was through, he'd been called to the ministry in this pleasant, coastal town. His initial interactions with the members of his new parish had been favorable. They had provided a small but adequate house for his use. He had moved Phebe and his orphaned nephew, Will Barrows, earlier in the week.

Phebe worked hard to get the little family settled while Joe worked on the first sermon he would ever deliver as a settled minister. He had been up late the night before putting the finishing touches on the sermon and praying for divine guidance during the upcoming service. Bolstered by a good breakfast, Joe felt as ready as he'd ever be to guide his new flock through the first service he was to share with them. Would to God it would be one of many Sabbaths he would share with the citizens of Kennebunkport. With a wife and child to support, Joe wanted to ensure they would always be provided for.

It was a thin line, he knew, between saying that which needed to be said and pushing the congregation so far that they would turn upon him. He had his own dear father's example of how a church can turn on a pastor. Reverend William Fessenden's Fryeburg congregation had bedeviled him to the point where he resigned and worked as a supply preacher until death took him at a young age. Other ministers he knew lived a hand-to-mouth existence if the church was not able to collect enough cash money to pay the preacher's meager salary. But no mind, the Gospel must be preached, and Joe knew his calling was strong to do so. He did worry sometimes that he had burdened Phebe too much by his call to serve. Better that she should have been the wife of a prosperous lawyer rather than reduced to extreme household economies. But Phebe was an enterprising housewife. He knew her sudden poverty as a child had given her insight and skills necessary to live as a parson's wife. Still, he would not ever have her lacking in basic comforts.

Joe reached up to help his wife down from the carriage. Then, he reached up for his lively nephew who was clamoring to be released to run with the other children until it was time for the long service ahead. With his wife's arm through his own, he walked to the front doors of the church. There they parted, Joe entering through the men's door and Phebe through the women's door, as was proper for Sunday morning. Joe walked down the aisle of the meeting house and sat down in the carved chair behind the pulpit, his head bowed in prayer. The bell rang out, calling the blessed to come to the seat of the Lord.

At the close of the service, Joe and Phebe stood at the back of the church, shaking hands and introducing themselves to the parishioners they had not yet met. All was pleasantness and calm with the sun shining in through the gracefully arched windows. The women issued kind invitations to Phebe to come and call upon them, and she returned the same. Plans were discussed for the upcoming church supper, and the men gathered outside discussing crops and horses. At last, the throng departed, and Joe and Phebe gathered up Will and returned home for the noon day meal Phebe had prepared the day before.

After dinner, Joe looked over his second sermon of the day, to be delivered at the evening service. Phebe sat with Will as he sounded out words in the Bible. The brief break between services passed most pleasantly in the small parsonage. Then, it was time to go back to the meeting house for the second sermon. Joe helped his wife and adopted son into the wagon, and they drove again to the meeting house door. Joe's second sermon seemed to be as well-received as his first.

At the end of the service, the family returned home. Joe ate a light supper and excused himself to bed. The laws of not working on the Sabbath did not pertain to ministers of the Gospel. Joe's first sermon of the day had lasted an hour and a half, his second nearly two hours. After all the preparation and delivery of two sermons, in addition to the other duties of two services and the constant demands of sociability and care of his parishioners, Joe felt quite exhausted. His day of rest would come on Monday, when all the rest of the world had returned to work.

Phebe gave Will a bowl of apples and fresh milk for his dinner. After tucking him into bed, she read to him the story of Noah and his ark filled with animals. When he had fallen asleep, she sat looking at his young face, reposed and peaceful in slumber. God had not seen fit to give her a babe of her own, but He had given her the care of this orphaned boy whose parents had died of scarlet fever within weeks of each other.

Will was gangly like a young puppy, working on growing into his feet. Oh, he was dear to her. As soon as they were well settled here, she would send to her mother for one or more of her brothers and sisters to join their household. Their young laughter would be most welcome in the quiet house, and they needed her as much as they ever did. Joe welcomed her family under their roof. She so wanted to have as many of her family as possible around their table. Their presence would help to fill the space in her heart left empty by her childless state. And perhaps, one day, God would answer her prayers for children of her own.

Kennebunkport, Maine

October 1821

Joe Fessenden poured a cup of coffee for his brother-in-law, Sam. Handing it to him, he said, "Your sister and I are worried about you."

"Worried?' queried Sam, "Why be worried about me?"

"You know you ever were one to fall into temptation where spirits are concerned. We hoped having you under our roof would help you to repent your loose living and learn to live a Godly life. A life your parents and your sister would be proud of."

Sam ducked his head. At eighteen, he was more and more feeling the constraints of living under his older sister's wing, and even more so his brother-in-law's stern reproofs. Still, he did not want to disappoint any of them. He'd tried to stay away from low companions, tried to go to church each Sunday, and live a Godly life. But, frankly, he felt more and more like he just wasn't cut out for polite society. He felt like a caged animal much of the time. Looking at his good brother-in-law, he said, "Joe, may I speak my mind to you?"

"Of course," Joe replied. "You must always feel as though you can. I am not unwise to the ways of young men. I did my share of sinful living before your sister turned me around."

Sam replied with a grin, "She is ever the reformer, my sister."

Joe laughed and slapped Sam lightly on the arm, "Now, tell me what's on your mind. It need go no further than between us, if that's your wish."

Sam took a deep breath, and as he started to speak, all his pent up dreams poured forth. "I have no desire to go to college or take up any trade but one. I have always known what I was to be. I want to be a sailor. I want to stand on the deck of a ship and look out over the ocean to the far horizon. If I have to stay on land one more day, I feel as though I will explode. I cannot speak of this to Phebe. She would have me lead a different life. And I fear it would kill my poor mother." He impatiently shoved his hands through his unruly hair. "Honest, Joe, I just don't know what to do. I just know

I can't be what everyone seems to want me to be."

Joe placed a steadying hand on his young brother's shoulder. "You know, Sam, I have ever felt a kinship with your family ever since I met you all in Canaan. And since the death of your dear father, I have felt myself to be both father and brother to you and your brothers and sisters. I would have you live a different life from what you want—a steady, predictable life, but you have ever been a free spirit. If this is the path you truly feel is the right one for you, I will talk to your sister for you, try to explain to her what it is to be a young man who must chart his own path."

Sam's face lit with joy. "Will you? Oh, that would be tremendous!"

Joe spoke up, saying, "Not so fast. I have a condition." Sam's face fell. "You must agree to wait six months and stay here with us and finish your studies."

Sam considered his options and decided six months of studies was a small price to pay for not having to face his sister and see the disappointment and worry on her face. Reaching out a hand, he warmly grasped that of Joe, saying, "Sir, you have a deal!"

Kennebunkport, Maine

April 1822

A westerly wind was blowing as the Cape Porpoise sailed out of Kennebunkport. Standing on deck, his feet firmly planted against the swaying of the deck, Sam Beach faced out toward the ocean. With his back to the shore, he could not see his sister wiping away her tears or his brother-in-law wrapping his arm around her to comfort her. Sam could still feel her tears, but staring out toward the horizon reminded him of what was ahead, rather than thinking of what he was leaving behind.

For six months, he did as promised, attending his studies with Joe, reading the Bible verses Phebe assigned him, going to church on Sunday, and staying away from companions who would lead him astray. For six months, he'd had no drop of liquor nor smoked even one cigar. He'd lived as a model citizen. And now, he was free. Truly free. Free to sail the world and see the sights he'd always dreamed of. This first voyage would take him to Boston and back to Kennebunkport. The next trip might take him still further.

His sister promised he would always have a home to return to when his ship was in port. It gave him some comfort knowing she would always be there for him. She had ever been a second mother to him and to all the children, especially since his father's tragic death. But for now, Sam was determined not to look back. His future lay before him, filled with excitement and adventure.

That night, several of his crewmates invited him to sit in on their poker game. He willingly accepted. In that spirit of comradeship, he joined them in a pint of grog and then another. Several hours later, he stumbled to his hammock reeking of cigar smoke and rum with his pockets empty. Clumsily climbing into his hammock, he was soon snoring in time to the rocking of the ship.

Kennebunkport, Maine

October 1823

Joe and Phebe walked down to the dock to see if Sammy's ship had come in on the high tide. He'd been gone six long months on this particular voyage. In the first few voyages, they'd seen a change come over him. No longer a slight boy with scrawny arms, Sam had filled out considerably with the hard work of sailing a ship. He was no longer an unsure youth. He'd developed a man's bluff and hearty mien and a sailor's deplorable habits. It was what Phebe had feared most, sending her brother off to sea. It put him in company with just the wrong element, allowing him to find companionship with intemperate men and females of dubious virtue. Her brother was becoming a hopeless reprobate.

She blamed Joe partially for the ruin of her brother. He supported Sam's wish to go to sea. But it was ever the place of the woman to set aside her own wishes in the face of male opposition. Phebe stood stiffly by Joseph's side, a frost in her tone and demeanor. Joe, for his part, felt to blame just as much as his wife did. He'd allowed his understanding of a young man's yearnings to undercut a minister's concern for that young man's eternal soul. Still, he could not but feel there was still hope to turn Sam from his worldly ways, to reach him in some way that would turn his path to righteous living.

Standing at the dock, Joe and Phebe could see the Cape Porpoise already docked. Scanning the faces at the deck railing, they looked for Sam. A figure on the gangplank waved to them. Sam trotted down the ramp, a seasoned sailor, carrying his duffel bag. Dropping it, he picked his sister up, twirling her around until she laughed out loud and demanded he release her. As she straightened her clothing and primly smoothed her hair, Sam shook Joe's hand vigorously. With Phebe between them, the two men set off for the parsonage with Sam regaling them with exaggerated stories of his travels.

That evening after dinner, Phebe gave Joe a pointed look and excused herself to the kitchen to clean up. Joe invited Sam into his study and shut the door. Sam looked at him with resignation. It was time, he supposed, for Joe to harangue him about his lack of virtuous living. He dreaded this part of every homecoming. Joe cleared his throat and fixed his gaze on Sam, a gaze that was both stern and kind. Sam saw there a reluctance on Joe's part to say what he needed to say, but also a determination to do his Christian duty by his brother.

Joe began his lecture as he always did, with a reminder of Sam's responsibility and debt to his dear mother and an admonishment of his sullying the memory of his departed father. Sam had heard it all before. He chafed under the constraints of a religious sense that he respected but simply could not live up to. He was destined to always fall short of the finer details of Christian duty. As Joe continued admonishing Samuel, he found himself getting hot under the collar. At last, Sam could stand it no more— the guilt, the recriminations, the expectations of his sister, her husband, his mother, and the uptight parishioners of his brother-in-law's parish. He abruptly stood up, saying, "I had planned to wait until my ship was sailing to tell you this. I've been offered a berth on another ship. I'll be first mate under a good captain."

Joe sat back in his chair. "I'm proud that you're making your way so well, Sam. Congratulations."

Before Joe could say more, Sam spoke up again. "The ship is out of Boston. I'll be leaving Kennebunkport."

Joe had a worried look on his face. "Your sister will not take this news well. "

"No," agreed Sam. "I thought to have you tell her."

Joe shook his head. "If you're man enough to sail as first mate, you're man enough to face your sister."

Sam gave a slight laugh, "I'm not so sure, Joe."

Joe grinned. "But, Sam, my concerns for you will be even greater now. You won't have your sister's steadying influence to guide you. You must be vigilant to protect your soul from these worldly transgressions. Will you promise me you'll have a care for your eternal soul? Will you seek to repent your wickedness and walk a better path?"

Sam replied, "I do try. The harder I try, the worse the temptations are that are put before me. But for my mother and my sister, I will always try to rise above the temptations. I promise you that." Clapping him on the back, Joe opened the door of his study, and the two men returned to the fireside where Phebe sat knitting stockings for young Will. Will rose up from playing with his kitten and climbed into Sam's lap, saying "Uncle Samuel, tell me a story."

Sam held his young nephew in his strong arms and began, "Well, Will, have I told you of the time my ship was becalmed off the North Carolina coast?" Will smiled and burrowed into his uncle's arms while, with wide eyes, he waited to hear what happened next.

Kennebunkport, Maine

March 1824

At cock's crow, Phebe forced herself to crawl out from underneath the thick quilts and away from the warmth of Joe's body. Swinging her feet over the edge of the bed, she glanced back at him with love and fondness. As she did, she saw on the sheets the unmistakable sign of her failure as a wife and as a woman.

Blood on the sheets. Her shoulders slumped and her face flushed hot with shame. Once again, she had failed to give Joe that which they both desired, a baby. Quickly pulling the covers up to hide her shame, she scurried from the room to clean herself up and dress for the day.

Later, after Joe left the house for the day, she would remove all trace of her failure. It was the same month after month. That which she desired and earnestly prayed for was not to be. Her own dear mother had succeeded in presenting her father with eleven babes, and she, Phebe, could not manage one. Determined to present a cheerful face at the breakfast table, Phebe splashed cold water on her face to wash away the tears. Later, as she scrubbed the sheets, she would give vent to her despair letting the salt of her tears wash away the stains.

Joseph came into the kitchen as Phebe stood with her back to the door, frying bacon. Going up behind her, he wrapped his arms around her, dropping a kiss on the top of her head. She did not respond, and he paused for a moment, confused. Phebe transferred the bacon from the frying pan onto a plate. Gently, Joseph touched her arm, turning her so he could see her face. "What is it, my dear?"

Phebe shook her head, and said, "Sit down, Joe, no sense in this breakfast getting cold."

He studied her face, trying to read it, casting about for some transgression he might have committed, some word he said that upset her, something he hadn't done that he had meant to do. "Please, won't you tell me what's wrong?" he asked.

Seeing his confusion, Phebe softened and said, "It is the usual trouble." And with that she burst into tears. He pulled her into his arms, holding tight, whispering calming words. She sobbed out,

"Why will God not give us even one babe. Just one. Is that so much to ask? I am half a woman, half a housewife, half a Christian, half a scholar. I can never seem to be all that I need to be." He held her still closer trying to absorb her pain into himself, to relieve her of her burden. Sobbing harder, Phebe choked on her words as she said, "I fail you over and over again."

With that, Joe held her out from his chest with his hands firmly on his shoulders. Urgently he said to her, "Stop that! You are the best gift God has ever given me. You have never failed me one single day of my life. If God chooses not to give us children, I will still be the happiest man in creation as long as you are by my side." Pulling her close again, he leaned down and whispered in her ear, "After all, my dear, if I have you and your mince pie, I'm far better off than most men in the parish." At that, Phebe gave a snort of laughter and slapped him lightly on the arm. Wiping her tears on her apron, the couple sat down next to each other, companionably leaning on each other's arm. Before Joe left the house, he took Phebe in his arms again, knowing how it was with her, giving her assurance she needed that she was loved and all was well.

Letter from Joseph Fessenden to Kennebunkport church

Sept. 20th 1829

To the congregation at church and society in Kennebunkport

Brothers and Friends,

For several years past, my situation has been, in some respects, peculiarly trying, notwithstanding the mercies with which I have been favoured. The local and other difficulties existing among us have embarrassed me not a little in my official duties and rendered, as it appears to my own mind, in a measure ineffectual the efforts which I have made to advance the cause of the Redeemer. Often, in consequence of these difficulties, have I had serious thoughts of requesting a dismission. Sometimes it has occurred to me, if I should leave you, you would be at liberty to obtain a minister in whom you would be united and who would, of course, be instrumental of good which I could never reasonably expect to accomplish. There again I have found, if I should go away, that it might open the door to the introduction of error and render your breach wide like the sea so that it could not be healed. To my friends who have been unwearied in their kindness to me, I am also strongly attached, and I have been unwilling to abandon my situation without reasons which would be satisfactory to them as well as to myself.

Thus I have continued with you, year after year, in a state of doubt and perplexity which, at times, has exceedingly depressed my spirits and made it difficult for me to perform as I ought or, as in other circumstances I might have done, the various and arduous labours of the ministry. But now the path of duty seems to me plain, and I have come to the conclusion, after seeking light from above and asking advice of friends, to request a dismission.

The principal reasons which have induced me to take this step I will briefly mention. Individuals in the church and town who possess wealth and influence and contribute liberally to the support of the Gospel have been for years, as I have reason to believe, dissatisfied with me and would prefer another minister. And I am perfectly convinced that this dissatisfaction while I continue as your pastor will not cease to exist. Others, both in the church and parish, have more recently become disaffected in consequence of the part I have acted in the unhappy dissentions which have prevailed in regard to our places of public worship and in consequence of my applying for the proceeds of the parsonage fund which I envisioned as belonging to me, while some contended that I had forfeited and even relinquished my claim to *this part of my support. Others again, as I am informed, object to the censures which the church has passed on some of her delinquent members.*

From these facts, it appears evident to my own mind that I cannot be so useful here as I might hope to be in some other part of the vineyard of our Lord, and that it is extremely desirable another man should be immediately procured who would not be likely to meet with the obstacles which I must inevitably encounter if I remain with you. I, therefore, ask my dismission and request the parish to grant it, and the church to unite with me, as soon as may be convenient, in calling a ministerial council for the purpose of dissolving the connection existing between us.

It will be recollected that one of the conditions of my settlement was, in case I wished for a dismission, I should be entitled to it by giving the parish six months notice. From this condition, I should esteem it a privilege to be excused, and desire to receive my dismission as soon as it can conveniently be obtained. With my request in this respect, the parish I doubt not will comply as it will be no advantage to them to avail themselves of the six months notice. Wishing you grace, mercy, and peace from God the Father and our Lord Jesus Christ, I subscribe myself your affectionate friend and pastor.

Joseph P. Fessenden

Phebe Beach Fessenden in Kennebunkport to Joseph Fessenden in Dixfield Oct. 3, 1829

My dearest husband,

I do sincerely thank you for your kind letter. I should have been very anxious, but Mr. Cummings told me the mail went from Portland to Dixfield the first of the week and returned the last. Therefore, I determined not to be anxious 'til Saturday, and this morning Willy, who has visited the office every day, brought me the treasure. You ask about my feelings after you left, dear husband. Mine were very distressing, especially when I came to our house, which looked desolate indeed. The good Colonel came in to see me, and looked as if he knew what sad things were fixing themselves in my heart! I have not seen one time since when I felt so perfectly bereaved as I did then.

I have been obliged to struggle against my feelings very much, for Mother has been in a perfect tease ever since you left, about going to Portland. And to preach patience to her, I must practice it myself. Brother Eben's daughter and Caleb, in one chaise, Tom and mother in another, started from here yesterday after an early dinner; the girls passed one night only here. I was disappointed in not seeing your brother. He is well. Brother Thomas has not returned yet. He may come this evening. 'Tis probable he may be waiting a day or two at Fryeburg for a private conveyance.

We have got on very well since you left; all been in as good health as usual. Mr. Cummings preached for us last Sabbath and preached well. In the morning from the passage, "How good and how pleasant it is for brothers to dwell together in unity, etc.;" afternoon, "Cast your burthens upon the Lord and he will sustain thee." The morning sermon was very suitable and excellent. In the evening from Luke 19th: 41-42. General doctrine, "Christ looks with grief and pity upon blinded, obstinate sinners, who disregard the things belonging to their eternal peace."

No movements have been made in the parish with which I am acquainted. I believe a parish meeting has been, or is to soon be called. John P. has done what he could to excite the feelings of the people against you by telling them that your going away is all a trick; that the object of it is to induce the people to leave the Unitarian preacher and when he is gone, you are coming back to sue them for the parsonage money and continue here as their minister to counteract the effect of this preacher. A parish meeting is concluded upon. 'Tis plainer now. This should have been done before you left; there is no attention to religion, not the least; the people are in a dreadful state.

I think we have reason for thankfulness that you are released from here and have a more interesting part of this vineyard to labour in. You wish I was with you—not more than I wish it, I assure you. The time seems long that I am to be separated from you. Do be careful of your health. I am rejoiced to learn you are labouring in the midst of consolation, instead of trials. O my dear husband, do pray for me, that I may be returned in my faith as a Christian. I greatly need your prayers and have no doubt I have them but don't pray for me as a backslider. Pray for me as an impenitent sinner. Our time in Kennebunkport amongst these thick-minded and shallow-headed people has led me to think ill of many, and I know this path does no good.

Would that your efforts in Dixfield may lead to our being settled with a new church so we can once again be together under one roof. Willy is well and sends you his love. He says to tell you he is taking good care of me in your absence.

The God of all grace be with you, your affectionate wife,

Phebe

Joseph Fessenden in Dixfield to Phebe Beach Fessenden in Kennebunkport

Oct. 12, 1829

My Dear Phebe,

I was exceedingly disappointed in not receiving a letter from you last Saturday and cannot conjecture a reason why you did not write. The mail comes to this place only once a week, and I shall be obliged to wait till next Saturday before I hear from you, and then perhaps I shall be disappointed again. I hope you and William are well. If I could only be assured that no evil had befallen you, I should be comparatively contented. But I will trust the same kind providence who has hitherto preserved us and will not, any further than I can help it, forebode trouble. If you were sick, my friends, I think, would not be so cruel as to delay informing me of it. I wrote you the first mail after my arrival, and you probably received the letter more than a week ago.

I have received another letter from Bridgton. They are solicitous that I should visit them as soon as possible, and I have engaged to be there the last Sabbath of this month. Of course, I shall remain here only one more Sabbath. If I hear from you next mail, and you are well, I shall not return home 'til after I have spent a Sabbath in Bridgton. If I hear that you are sick, I shall return immediately. If I hear nothing, I shall hardly know what to do.

The people in this place need a minister exceedingly. But they are feeble and cannot without foreign aid support one. When I leave them, some one I hope will be procured to take my place at least for a few weeks. There is an ordination at Weld, a town fifteen miles distant from this on Wednesday. I purpose to attend it.

And then I expect to meet Dr. Gillett, Mr. Thurston, and other trustees of the minister's association. With them, I will intercede for Dixfield and trust that further assistance may be rendered to this little flock of Christ.

I was informed the other day that the church and people at the Port had sent for Mr. Lowe of Andover and that he was to be with them yesterday. The people in this region speak well of Mr. L., and I hope if it please the Lord that he may suit and become their pastor. The good work here is still going on, though it has met with a check in consequence of the wicked conduct of Sectarians. Calvinists, Baptists, Universalists, and Unitarians all join hands in opposing it.

On the Sabbath before last, a man was immersed. The first that ever was immersed, I believe, in this place, and a Baptist preacher delivered a discourse on the occasion on "the only mode of baptism." Plunging over head and ears, the object, I have no doubt, was to draw the attention of the young converts to the mode of baptism, and if possible, get them underwater. But they all, as yet, stand firm, and I pray that they may continue to do so. In the forenoon of the Sabbath, I hear mentioned a Unitarian preached and the Baptist minster and the man who was to be plunged and Universalists composed his audience. It requires the patience of Job to bear with persons who conduct in such a manner in time of revival. But the Lord reigns, let the earth rejoice. Christ says, "All that my Father hath given me shall come unto me." This is a blessed promise.

I promised, if I remember right, in my last to give you a more particular account of the work of grace here when I wrote again. But as I hope to see you soon I shall keep particulars 'til we meet. Providence permitting, I will finish my letter when I return from ordination.

Wednesday Oct. 14

I returned from ordination this evening. It has been an interesting day to me. Mr. Thurston made the ordaining prayer. It both shared and melted my soul. He is indeed a godly man. Father Sewall I saw. His countenance is as mild and placid as ever. My health is good. I rode 20 miles yesterday in the saddle and walked two. Today I have walked four and rode fifteen. So you perceive I am active and do not spare my body. I hope, too, I enjoy my mind, if I am not deceived. I have some precious seasons of sweet contemplation with my Saviour.

May the Lord bless you, my dearest, with the light of his countenance. Tell brother Sam if he is with you that "now" is the accepted and NOW the day of Salvation. If he intends ever to repent and come to Christ, he must begin this great work without delay and in earnest. O pray for him, for his soul while he yet is on the brink of ruthless ruin. Give my love to him and solemnly warn him from me to escape immediately from the wrath to come and lay hold of eternal life. Tell dear William, too, his soul is precious. Kiss him for me and tell him to repent and give his heart to Christ. I feel enough for the church and people in Kennebunkport. It is my prayer that they may be visited with the salvation from evil. Remember me affectionately to my friends.

Goodbye, my dearest. I long to see you and hope I shall in a fortnight. May God preserve, protect and bless you!

Your very affectionate,

JP Fessenden

South Bridgton, Maine

December 23, 1829

The old man's breath rattled in his throat. Parson Joe prayed aloud for the deliverance of his immortal soul while the man's children gathered close to his bedside. His daughters, Nancy and Rebecca held each other, crying quietly. Nancy's husband Dr. Reuel Barrows held his father-in-law's wrist in his hand, feeling a faint pulse still flickering. The man's strong sons, John and Thomas stood as sentinels on either side of their father's bedstead. The man called out suddenly and strongly, raising his head from the bed, "My sons, hear this, my last wish." Gasping, he collapsed again as John and Thomas leaned in.

"Yes, Sir," spoke John, the eldest. Gasping for breath, the man spoke. "Increase the amount I left to the new church to $5,000." With that, the man sank into an unconscious state from which he would not return.

Parson Joe Fessenden, newly ordained to lead the South Parish church just two days before, was already faced with the difficult task of laying to rest the new church's founding father and one of the area's leading citizens. Squire Enoch Perley, a man of such stature that though he was of a small frame physically, his character cast a tall shadow. The parson carefully closed the staring blue eyes of the Old Squire, praying for his family who had not yet grasped the depth of their loss. Rebecca Fessenden spoke to her sister, Nancy, "Oh, Nancy, what will we ever do without him?"

Nancy replied, "He's with Ma'am now. We can find comfort in that. He missed her so after she passed." The sisters wrapped their arms around each other while Thomas put a comforting arm around them.

Christmas Eve dawned in sadness at the Perley homestead. With their father's body at rest in the parlor awaiting the funeral service, a pall hung over the household. Tom Perley stood looking at his father's Bible, open still upon the table where the old gent had left it just days before. Enoch Perley's spectacles lay where he left them, folded on the Bible that for so many years he had held up as he read to his family in the evenings. Glancing at the open page to see what his father had been reading, Tom saw his father's favorite passage from Ecclesiastes, "to every thing there is a season." How like his father to be thinking of the ending of his life as a passing of the season. A lifelong farmer, his father did everything in its proper season.

The sound of the front door opening caused Tom to glance up. His brother John was returning from the barn and in his company was Parson Joe Fessenden. John was speaking to the parson as he came through the door, "I appreciate you coming to call, Parson. We need to arrange for Sir's funeral service."

"Of course, of course," said the parson.

Tom spoke up saying, "I have a verse for you that I think speaks to my father's life and character. I found it here in his Bible, the last page he ever read from." The details of the service were discussed and the time of the funeral service set for the day after Christmas at the South Parish church. Without having to ask for assistance, the family knew that neighbors and friends would prepare food for the family and the funeral. The church would need to be heated and opened up, but again, no word need be spoken to cause that to happen. Folks in the parish knew what to do in times of trouble. Only by relying on one another could they survive in the often harsh conditions of living in the Maine woods.

After consoling the family with prayers, Parson Joe returned to his waiting carriage and headed back to his temporary lodgings at his Cousin Jonathan's house. Shutting himself into the bedroom he occupied, he began to write the funeral sermon for Squire Enoch Perley.

In the afternoon on December 26th, a stream of carriages, buggies, and horses passed by Jonathan Fessenden's house on the way to the church, diagonally across from his house. The family wrapped themselves against the cold and walked to the church. Parson Joe was already there, standing with the Perley family with a warm welcome for all who came to bid farewell to a great man. Humble farmers, town fathers, business partners, church members from the new church, members from the original church, cousins, nieces and nephews, merchants, and friends all crowded into the small church until all the pews were filled, and the aisles were packed by the overflow throng. The weak winter sun gleamed through the windows of the church, lighting on the faces of the assembled congregation. At the appointed time, Parson Joseph Fessenden looked out over his new flock and began to speak to them.

"Dearly Beloved, We are gathered here today to lay to rest a respected and loved member of this community. It is a sad day for us all and a difficult day especially for the children of this great man. It is good for us to gather here to show our respect for this man, to comfort his grieving family, and to draw together as a community of neighbors and Christians. Squire Enoch Perley served as an example to us all of a man who took all the talents and gifts given to him by birth and hard work and used them for the good of his family and his neighbors. The Squire's children have asked me to share with you the Squire's best loved verses from the Bible, and indeed, the last verses he read before succumbing to the fate we all must meet before we can be reunited with our Holy Father and the loved ones who have preceded us on that journey.

Reading from Ecclesiastes:

'To every thing there is a season, and a time to every purpose under the heaven:

A time to be born, and a time to die; a time to plant, and a time to pluck up that which is planted;

A time to kill, and a time to heal; a time to break down, and a time to build up;

A time to weep, and a time to laugh; a time to mourn, and a time to dance;

A time to cast away stones, and a time to gather stones together; a time to embrace, and a time to refrain from embracing;

A time to get, and a time to lose; a time to keep, and a time to cast away;

A time to rend, and a time to sew; a time to keep silence, and a time to speak;

A time to love, and a time to hate; a time of war, and a time of peace.

What profit hath he that worketh in that wherein he laboureth?

I have seen the travail, which God hath given to the sons of men to be exercised in it.

He hath made every thing beautiful in his time; also he hath set the world in their heart, so that no man can find out the work that God maketh from the beginning to the end.

I know that there is no good in them, but for a man to rejoice, and to do good in his life.

And also that every man should eat and drink, and enjoy the good of all his labour, it is the gift of God.

I know that, whatsoever God doeth, it shall be for ever; nothing can be put to it, nor any thing taken from it; and God doeth it, that men should fear before him.

That which hath been is now; and that which is to be hath already been; and God requireth that which is past.

And moreover I saw under the sun the place of judgment, that wickedness was there; and the place of righteousness, that iniquity was there.

I said in mine heart, God shall judge the righteous and the wicked; for there is a time there for every purpose and for every work.

I said in mine heart concerning the estate of the sons of men that God might manifest them, and that they might see that they themselves are beasts.

For that which befalleth the sons of men befalleth beasts; even one thing befalleth them; as the one dieth, so dieth the other; yea, they have all one breath; so that a man hath no preeminence above a beast, for all is vanity.

All go unto one place; all are of the dust, and all turn to dust again.

Who knoweth the spirit of man that goeth upward, and the spirit of the beast that goeth downward to the earth?

Wherefore I perceive that there is nothing better, than that a man should rejoice in his own works; for that is his portion; for who shall bring him to see what shall be after him?'"

Freedom's Light
Inaugural Edition, Portland, Maine

January 7, 1837

Rights for All! The National Shame That Lives Beneath Freedom's Wing!

"We hold these truths to be self evident, that ALL men were created equal." So said Thomas Jefferson at the founding of this great republic. These great words resounded across the globe and within the hearts and souls of all men. To determine the paths of our lives, to ensure our own futures through hard work, to sleep safely in our own homes, to chose a life's mate, to raise our children, to be treated fairly and justly by the law, these are the rights of man. Yet here beneath freedom's wing more than two million of our brethren are held in abject slavery.

Forced to live unnatural lives and denied BY LAW the most basic human rights. The fruits of their backbreaking labor go to their masters. They have no freedom to walk about the land, subject always to the will of their masters. Their marriages are not recognized in the eyes of the law. Their wives or husbands may be sold away at the whim of the master. Their children are not theirs to raise. They, too, may be sold away to cover a master's debts. Their women are subject always to the will of the master and let no man dare to stand up to the tyranny to protect his family for fear of swift and cruel reprisal.

This is the lot of our dark skinned brethren. It is the shame of this great nation to allow such calumny against liberty to exist within its borders. We endeavor here to give some small service to the ending of all such impurities that stain the reputation of this great land. For our brothers and sisters in chains, we stand ready to aid you, to welcome you, to fight for your freedom, and to lift you up to full citizenry. While the cruel boot of the master is upon you, we will give you your voice until, as our New England poet says,

"When, smitten as with fire from heaven,

The captive's chains shall sink in dust,

And to his fettered soul be given

The glorious freedom of the just!"

South Bridgton, Maine

March 1835

After five long years of temporary housing arrangements, Phebe Fessenden was finally going home. Home to her very own house, planned with her needs and the needs of her family in mind. Climbing down from the carriage with the help of her husband, she stood looking around the dooryard of her new home. The grounds were still rough from the construction of the house, littered with sawed off board ends and plowed up dirt. She ignored the rough edges and looked instead at the house. Her very own house. The house where she and Joe would make a life for themselves and for their children, should they by God's blessing ever have any of their own.

Joe's nephew Will Barrows jumped down from the wagon that held all their worldly goods. He ran off to explore the barn, his joy at having a new home was evident in the cartwheel he turned in the dooryard. The house was strong and well-proportioned. Freshly clapboarded, the shutters not yet put up; the house seemed to welcome its new inhabitants. Joe came up behind Phebe and wrapped his arms around her waist. Leaning down, he whispered in her ear, "Welcome home, my love, welcome home."

After all the troubles of the church in Kennebunkport, and moving from pillar to post in South Bridgton, both were looking forward to a peaceful life in their own place. Nearly fifteen years of marriage to a country parson had taught Phebe to take life as it came. But, to have her own house, one not owned by the church— to be able to plant asparagus and an apple tree and still be there when it was ready for harvesting, to Phebe, it was indeed a blessing of the first order.

Taking Phebe by the hand, Joe led her to the gracious front entryway. He picked her up into his arms and stepped up on the granite steps. Phebe laughed out loud, a sound he had not heard very often of late. He carried her over the new threshold, grinning broadly, his blue eyes twinkling. Taking her into the formal parlor to the right of the entry, he deposited her gently in the empty room and stood back to watch her as she looked around her new home.

Phebe went first to the fireplace, running her hand across the smooth wood. She turned about, inspecting the windows. Then, she proceeded across the hall to the family parlor and then on to the kitchen with its shining new hand pump bringing water directly to the kitchen sink. From there, she stepped into the pantry, looking at the new shelves, bare and waiting for her preserves and pickles. Joe followed her from room to room watching her reaction, wanting so much for her to be pleased.

She walked back through the house to the staircase with the beautifully-carved newel post. Walking up the stairs, she inspected the bedrooms one by one, looking out each window at the view. Standing in the front bedroom on the south side of the house, Phebe stood looking out the window to the pond just across the way. The sun shone on her dark hair, lighting up the red and gold lights. She turned to Joseph with a smile, saying, "Husband, we are home at last." Joe laughed out loud, grabbing her by the waist and spinning her around in a heady, joyful dance. "Joe! What will your parishioners think of such actions!" she cried out, laughing.

"Let them think I love my wife!" Joe replied.

South Bridgton

April 1835

The church bell pealed out, calling the faithful of South Bridgton to worship. The early-birds had already taken their seats and sat staring stoically ahead. Parson Joe glanced toward Deacon Peabody who checked his time piece. It was a beautiful April day and temperatures were surprisingly warm. Parson Joe shook his head. His parishioners might need another reminder of the Lord's injunction to remember the Sabbath and keep it holy. On a warm spring day like this, turn-out was apt to be lower than usual. It was unfortunate, since the parson had an important message planned.

Deacon Peabody stepped to the front of the church to lead the singing of the opening hymn. He sang the first line, and the congregation repeated it and followed thus through the hymn. Standing behind the pulpit, Parson Joe began the service with an opening prayer. The congregation settled in for what would, if history was any indication, be a very long sermon. Parson Joe was known for his ability to deliver long sermons, and he did so twice every Sunday, delivering one sermon in the morning and the other in the late afternoon. With all the anti-slavery talk in the section, members of the congregation had an inkling of what this morning's sermon might entail. The families who were in attendance sat each in their own pew, bought and paid for and handed down from generation to generation. Heaven help the uninitiated who sat in the wrong pew.

Parson Joe stood tall in the pulpit and began reading from the folded over manuscript he'd prepared during the week.

"Ephesians 5:11 Have no fellowship with the unfruitful works of darkness, but rather reprove them."

After reading the opening verse, he set about instructing his congregation on the importance of reproving those who do wrong. He hit upon his favorite subjects with great vigor—the evils of rum-drinking and the heresy of the Catholics. Then, as expected, he began to speak about the evils of slavery, saying:

"I must notice the awful sin of slavery as a work of horrid darkness which we must all unite in reproving. But what is the sin of slavery as it actually exists in our country? Yes. What is it? This question needs to be asked by at least four fifths of the northern states for, as yet, they know not what American slavery is. Although it sits as an incubus upon them and like a millstone hung about the necks of the nation is ready to sink it into the grief of perdition. Although we groan under its weight daily, and by it the chariot wheels of our national prosperity are taken off, so that we are ready to be overwhelmed by the waves of divisive wrath; yet, as a community, we know not what it is. And are we then to blame? And why not?

Will the murderer plead justification in the courts of his country and at the bar of God because forsooth he was ignorant of the law, 'Thou shalt not kill?' 'For this they willingly are ignorant of' in reference to another subject, and so it may be said of us with the utmost propriety in relations to American slavery. This nation is most strangely infatuated, and it will be a miracle of mercy if we are not destroyed.

The beacon set off in the fate of Egypt and Babylon and other nations of antiquity whom God destroyed for their sins of oppression is not heeded by us at all. One of the most enormous national sins of which a nation was ever guilty since the foundation of the world, is the sin of this nation in holding more than two million of their own countrymen in chains.

What makes this sin more aggravating in us is our pretention to liberty and equal rights, and of extending to all good citizens the inalienable rights of life, liberty, and the pursuit of happiness. This day one sixth part of the whole population of these United States who have not forfeited their liberty for any crime whatever are held as goods and chattels. Yes, from the moment they first draw the vital air until they cease to breathe, slavery holds them in its inexorable, withering, hope-killing grasp. They are born slaves; they drag out a miserable existence in slavery and die without ever tasting the sweets of liberty.

They are sold at auction and at private sale like dumb beasts, and at the will of their masters under the hammer of the auctioneer. The dearest ties of relationship are severed while parents and children, husbands and wives, brothers and sisters are torn from the embraces of each other by the ruthless hand of tyranny and oppression. The fountains of knowledge to them are locked up, and they are forbidden under the severest penalty to learn to read the word of God.

Tortures a thousand times more excruciating than immediate death are inflicted upon them in numberless instances, until the fields and plains of free America, whence sounds the voice of liberty, is drenched and stained with their tears and blood. Long have they groaned and cried and bled, but the heart of America has not relented. When with uplifted manacled hands, on their bended knees with tears of anguish rolling down their cheeks, they call on us to pity them, saying, 'Are we not men and brethren?'

We drive them from our presence with the cart whip, and load them with imprecations, curses, and increased misery. For daring to ask of us mercy, all this we do and ten thousand times more than can ever be told this side of the judgment seat, while at the same moment we hold in our hand the declaration of our independence, declaring that God hath made all men equal--and THE BIBLE which declares, that 'God hath made of our blood all nations of men,' and 'that he is no respecter of persons.'

Nor does the sin of slavery lie exclusively at the door of the slaveholding states. Yet multitudes are endeavoring to silence the thunderings of conscience and the wailings of suffering humanity with this delusion. Do they not know that the body of this death is bound to all the states by the strong cords of national compact? Of this they can hardly, in the utmost stretch of charity be thought ignorant, for the moment we say any thing to them on the subject of emancipation, they reply that we have no constitutional right to interfere with the subject—we have guaranteed the right to the Southern states to hold slaves.

Here, then, is a tacit acknowledgment that we are all involved in the guilt of slavery—that we, in forming our national compact, traded in the bodies and souls of men. Yes, to perpetuate our liberty, we bartered away the liberty, happiness, and lives of millions of our brethren! And there we hold them.

Does not every person at the north know that if a fugitive slave in flying from the yoke of his oppressor's lands in Maine or in any other non-slaveholding state, the civil authority is bound to deliver him up at the request of his pretended owner? And does he not know that if the slaves in the south were to arise in vindication of their inalienable rights, we are bound to march from the north, sword in hand, to maintain the heaven-insulting claims of slaveholders and tighten more severely the chains of the oppressed?

And yet nothing is more common at the North than to hear the sentiment expressed that we have nothing to do with the sin of slavery. This plea will not stand in the court of heaven, before the God of the oppressed. As a nation, we are guilty, and as a nation we are called upon to repent. Every individual has some thing to do. At least, let him clean the stains from his own garments. We call not for physical resistance to the constitution or laws but for the men of this land, especially for Christians and Christian ministers, to wage an uncompromising war with this sin by declaring the testimony of God and wielding those spiritual weapons which are mighty through God to the pulling down of the strongholds of Satan.

What can we infer from a proper view of the divine perfections for the past dispensations of Providence but speedy destruction to this nation unless they listen to the cries of their enslaved and oppressed brethren. Let them go free!

We are astonished at the unreasoning of Pharaoh, yet we are following in his steps. We speak contemptuously of God and bury his holy law beneath our feet. We tear down and ridicule the workmanship of his hands in degrading the poor black man and throw insult in the face of the Almighty by refusing the granting of equality to our colored brethren who bear his image. Ah! Will not God cure himself of his adversaries? Will not his soul be avenged on such a nation as this?

Yes, verily, except they repent, although 'thou hast said in thine heart, I will ascend into heaven, I will exalt my throne above the stars of God; I will sit also upon the mount of the congregation in the sides of the north; I will ascend above the heights of the clouds; I will be like the most High; yet thou shalt be brought down to hell, to the sides of the pit.' Oh! My heart sickens and bleeds when I contemplate this and other black and God-provoking sins of my country, and I feel as if I could wish to raise my voice to a tone of remonstrance which would be heard in every dwelling throughout the land. Repent, or the judgments of offended heaven will descend and consume us.

See you not the clouds arising?
Dread you not the coming storm?
Zion's watchmen, sound the trumpet,
Ere we lie, like Samson, shorn.

Christians to your hiding place,
Keep you near the throne of grace.
See, oh see! The storm is hasting.
Clouds are blackening all the sky;

Hear, oh hear the mighty rushing-
Christians wake! Or you must die.
Flee you to the King of kings,
Take your succor 'neath his wings.

See! The lightning's fitful gleam
Like the lurid flames below;
Hear the dismal night bird's scream
Fearfully, foreboding woe

Christians, wake! How can you sleep?
Wake! Or this land the storm will sweep!

And can you do nothing by way of rebuking the God-provoking sin of slavery? No. You can do something. Although you cannot see the slaveholder and depict to him in person his crimson guilt and call for him as he hopes for the mercy of God and wishes to avoid the pains of hell hereafter, to unclench his iron grasp from the throats of his unoffending colored brethren; you can see all around you aiders and abettors of the unrighteous system at the north, and to these you can do your duty. You can do your part to waken up a general indignation against this crying abomination. And you can speak to the slaveholder, too and carry conviction to his conscience, if not by word of mouth, yet by giving your name and influence to anti-slavery societies who bear their open testimony against his wickedness.

Testimony of this description, through the public press, meets his eye almost every day and makes him tremble in view of his guilt and a judgment to come. You can speak also to slaveholders in very state. Where your fellow creatures, the down-trodden poor of Christ's purchase, are groaning under the cruel yoke of oppression, by signing memorials, protesting against the sin of slavery, and praying the national legislature to remove it, to cause it at once to cease, from the District of Columbia and other portions of territory where it exists, over which Congress has exclusive and unlimited jurisdiction. Oh, let not the churches at the north imagine that they cannot, if they wanted, effectually reprove slaveholders and slave holding all over the union. This moral power is immense.

And if they were awoken to the subject and united and should put forth all their efforts, the giant sin of slavery would receive a fatal wound and soon expire. It is in the moral power of the churches at the north under God to remove speedily this hateful evil of the land. And if they do it not, and the evil be continued 'til the judgments of the Almighty descend and the country is destroyed, they will be the guilty cause of this ruin, and the blood of oppressed millions will in this great day be found upon their shirts.

You know your duty. I have only to say then, be strong and do it."

Parson Joe looked out from under his brushy eyebrows to see if he had hit his target with the message. He saw several of the women crying, the children were all stark upright in the pews, and a couple of the men had thunderous scowls upon their faces.

Parson Joe bowed his head in prayer, exhorting his congregation to do all they could to end the evils of man's depravity and to reprove those who do wrong. Following an emphatic Amen by the parson, a few halfhearted Amens were heard from the congregation. Deacon Peabody set about collecting the offering and followed up with the closing hymn.

Speaking to the parson after church, Deacon Peabody said quietly, "I think you stirred some of the wrong people today, Parson."

With a half a smile, the parson replied, "I did what needed to be done." Picking up his Bible and his sermon, he stopped at the family pew to collect his wife, niece, and nephew. They walked down the hill together to enjoy Sunday dinner before resting for the evening service.

Luray, Virginia

August 1837

Sadie groaned as another contraction wrapped its hard arms around her midsection. Beads of sweat dotted her ebony skin in the confines of the airless cabin. Twisting on the tattered coverlet on the packed dirt floor, Sadie gasped out, "Mauma! Will it come soon?"

Strong, soothing hands straightened her twisted body, murmuring, "Soon, girl. In God's time."

As the contractions grew stronger, Sadie panted in the heat, moaning. "Lord, deliver me!" she cried out in agony. "Jesus, save me!"

"You push now, girl, push that chile into this mean ole world," urged Mauma.

Bearing down, straining, Sadie pushed her child into Mauma's waiting hands. Lying back, she gasped out, "Is Massa's chile a boy or a girl?"

Mauma carefully wiped the babe down with a rag and responded, "Dat your chile, not Massa's. You has a girl chile, honey. A strong, fine girl chile." The babe squirmed in Mauma's arms, legs moving. "Oh, looka her little legs go. Dis chile gonna travel far. She gonna travel far." Mauma handed the baby to Sadie who held her close to her breast. "What you gwine name that girl chile," asked Mauma.

Sadie held the baby close, stroking one rough finger down the soft baby cheek. "Oh, she a beauty, Mauma. She need a beautiful name. I'm a gonna call her Mathilde after your mama." The baby cuddled in closer, opening her blue eyes, and following the sound of her mother's voice.

The next day, Sadie hung the child in a sling around her chest and returned to work in the plantation kitchen. Dulcie, the cook, smiled broadly at Sadie when she walked through the door, slightly hunched over, still aching from the birth. "Why, girl, you look downright peaked. You sit down, and I get the tray ready for Missus this morning. Now let me get a look at that babe of your'n. Lawd! She a beauty!" Leaning her grizzled head close to Sadie, taking in the sweet scent of the newborn, she said sadly, "Oh, I do miss my own chillun. Massa didn't let me keep a one of mine. You keep yours close as long's you can. A mother sure do grieve somethin awful when dey gone."

Dulcie wiped away her tears and began preparing the breakfast tray for Missus. She put Missus' toast on one of her best china plates and her tea in a delicate china cup adding a fresh sprig of fragrant white jasmine. When it was ready, she told Sadie to sit tight. Dulcie lifted the tray, and moving heavily, she left the kitchen and slowly climbed the back staircase.

Knocking lightly, she entered Missus' bedroom, greeting her with a calm, "Good morning, Missus."

Her mistress lay wanly on her piled up pillows, her dressing gown did not hide the thin, wasted frame beneath it. Ellen Pendergast had not recovered well from her last pregnancy. Her babe had lasted just two hours before his breath stopped. He joined two brothers and a sister in the family graveyard. She greeted Dulcie listlessly asking, "Where has Sadie got to? Why isn't she bringing my tray?"

Dulcie replied, "Missus, Sadie done have her baby yesterday."

Mrs. Pendergast looked quizzically at Dulcie, "That was yesterday. I gave her the day off to have her baby. Where is she today? She is the only one who can fix my bath the way I like it! You tell her I need her back right away."

"Yassum, I tell her you lookin for her."

Dulcie left the bedroom and trudged down the steps, muttering under her breath, "Missus been abed fo' three month after her poor chile been borned. Colored girl got to be back to work same day. Got no time for proper restin'. No time for coddlin'." She got up a full head of steam on her way back to the kitchen. Sadie looked up from nursing her babe when Dulcie came in. "Missus want you to fix her bath. Say nobody do it good like you. You gwine have to go. Don't be taking that baby wit you. Missus don't want to see what Massa been up to while she laid low."

Taking the baby from Sadie, Dulcie held the child to her ample bosom, rocking her and crooning to her. Sadie squared her shoulders and heaved a sigh, forcing a smile to her face. She went upstairs to the bedroom and knocking gently, she entered. "Missus need her bath drawn now?" she asked.

"Yes, Sadie. Where have you been?" the mistress asked petulantly. "Dulcie brought my tray this morning. She is so old and slow that by the time it arrives from the kitchen my toast is cold."

"Yes, Missus, sorry for that, Missus. I here now to take care of you." Sadie placed towels on the floor and shoved the heavy metal tub into the sunshine. Grasping her tender midsection, she returned to the kitchen to fetch two house slaves to help her carry the hot water up the stairs. With the tub filled and steam rising, she helped Mrs. Pendergast into the tub, handing her soap and her wash cloth. When Mrs. Pendergast was through bathing, Sadie helped her rise and step out of the tub, holding her towel ready for her.

As Mrs. Pendergast dried herself, she glanced toward Sadie and took a sharp intake of breath. Angrily she pointed toward Sadie's bare legs. "What is that!?"

Sadie looked down and saw streaks of blood running down the insides of her legs. "Oh, Missus, I'm sorry. I don't know what the matter with me."

Mrs. Pendergast replied, "You're getting blood all over my floor. Get that cleaned up immediately!" Sadie was shaking hard, not knowing why she was bleeding and horrified at what Mrs. Pendergast might do to punish her. She took a kitchen rag from her pocket and mopped up the blood on the floor as best she could. Her breath came in frightened sobs. She feared she was dying. "Get out!" shouted Mrs. Pendergast. "Disgusting darky! Get out!" Sadie clutched her dress and the kitchen rag, cramming both between her legs, desperately trying not to bleed on Missus' floor. She ran from the room and down to the kitchen, terrified and whimpering.

Dulcie looked up from peeling potatoes and saw the state Sadie was in. She put down the paring knife and reached for the frightened girl. "Sadie, what wrong? You hurt?" Looking at her hard, Dulcie realized Sadie was bleeding from the birth of the baby. Taking Mathilde into one arm and putting the other arm around Sadie, Dulcie led them to the well outside the kitchen door. Letting go of Sadie, Dulcie filled the water bucket for her. She spoke to Sadie soothingly, "Here, you clean yourself up good. That baby done tore you up some, that's all. You gonna be jes' fine. You working too hard too soon. That's all. You gonna be jes' fine. Jes' fine. And you got a fine baby girl to show for all yo troubles."

Gradually, Sadie's breathing slowed. She rinsed out the worst of the blood from her clothes. Standing in the hot sun would soon dry them. She wiped her tears and reached for her baby. "Mathilde," she breathed her baby's scent in and, uncovering a breast, began to feed the baby.

***

Matt McGillian rang the summoning bell in the side yard of the plantation. In the relative cool of the evening, most of the slaves were sitting in front of their cabins resting after a day in the tobacco fields. Hearing the bell, they glanced at each other nervously. To be summoned at this time of day meant only bad news for a slave. They made their way to the side yard where the overseer stood, still ringing the bell.

Someone in the crowd of slaves let out a gasp and all eyes turned to the form at the feet of the overseer. Young Cassio. Missing from the tobacco fields for three days now. His once strong and supple frame was bent at an odd angle and the side of his face was smashed in. He lay insensate on the ground. McGillian spoke out loudly so all the slaves could hear. "This here is what's left of Cassio. He thought he'd be clever and make a run for it. He spent two nights in the hills. We went after him with bloodhounds, and they found him holed up in a thicket. Your master and I don't take kindly to property running off like that. Now, you're gonna see what happens to runaways."

He leveled a kick at Cassio's side. "Get up, nigger." Cassio lay where he'd fallen. "I said, get up, nigger." The mass of bloody flesh began slowly to move. Cassio struggled slowly to his feet, dazedly looking around. He found his mother, Gertie, in the crowd and stared into her eyes. Gertie returned his hard gaze, holding back her sobs, standing close to Dulcie who held her up. Sadie stood close by, clutching Mathilde to her chest trying to shield her from the violence and the grief.

Grasping Cassio by the arm, McGillian half dragged him to the whipping post, tying his hands and tearing away the remnants of his shirt. Stepping back, McGillian picked up his whip. "This is what we do to niggers that run away." Pulling back his arm, he arced the whip and unloaded it with a strong slap onto Cassio's back. Cassio cried out, and Gertie gasped hard, clinging to Dulcie's arm. Pulling his arm back, McGillian lashed again. The impact of the whip sent blood spattering into the air. Again and again, McGillian worked the whip. After the first dozen stripes, Cassio fell silent, slumped against the post. When McGillian had delivered forty lashes, he calmly rolled up his whip and turned and walked away.

The slaves stood silently watching him until he entered the main house. When it was safe, Gertie rushed to Cassio with two of the male slaves. One cut the rope that kept Cassio upright. The other helped Gertie lower Cassio to the ground. Gertie looked into his eyes and began to sob. His head lolled to the side with his lifeless eyes open to the blue sky. All night long the slave quarters were filled with the keening grief of a mother whose only son had been taken from her.

With the sounds of Gertie's grief echoing from the cabin next door, Sadie held her newborn close, sitting on the hard ground in the cabin she shared with her mother. She rocked the baby and whispered to her the words Mauma had spoken when Mathilde was born, "My chile gonna travel far. My chile gonna be free." She sang softly to the baby with a mother's desperate tears running down her face,

"On my way to Canaan land
I'm on my way, well, to Canaan land
On my way, oh yes, Canaan land
On my way, glory hallelujah, I'm on my way

I had a mighty hard time
But I'm on my way
Had a mighty hard time
Well, well, well, on my way
Mighty hard time on my way
On my way, glory hallelujah, on my way

Well I'm on my way, oh to Canaan land
Well I'm on my way, oh to Canaan land
On my way, Canaan land
On my way, glory hallelujah, I'm on my way"

Phebe Beach Fessenden in South Bridgton, Maine to Samuel Beach in Savannah, Georgia

October 16, 1837

My dear brother,

You asked especially that I write to you of how your wife and daughter are faring since coming to stay with us. My little namesake is thriving. At three months old, she is growing strong and perfectly healthy. She is a happy baby, cheerful and sweet. Little Phebe is loved by us all. Mary cuddles her like a doll and enjoys rocking her to sleep and dressing her each morning. My husband spoils both the girls terribly. He loves them to distraction.

Your wife does not fare as well. As you know from our previous letters, we were concerned that Sarah would not be happy here in the country. She was raised a city girl, and I fear she misses the noise and the excitement. She will not be content to stay here for long I think. We are most concerned as to what you would have us do about the child should your wife decide to leave us. We would not want to separate a mother from her babe. You must be very clear with us what you would have us do should Sarah leave.

Your wife and child are welcome to stay with us for as long a time as pleases all, but we fear more and more that Sarah will not remain much longer. Joe asks very particularly for you to say what we are to do for you in regards to the child should your wife desire to return to her family in Boston.

Your affectionate sister,

Phebe B. Fessenden

Freedom's Light
Portland, Maine

November 20, 1837

Rights for All

Hero and Martyr! Shocking Murder of Maine Man Fighting in the Cause of Liberty!

News reached this office today of the shocking murder on the seventh day of this month of Elijah Lovejoy, a newspaper editor from Maine. Lovejoy, a staunch abolition man, was defending his printing press from a vicious mob in Alton, Illinois. His building was set afire, and as he ran out of the burning building, he was wantonly shot to death in cold blood. Lovejoy, who was born in Albion, went west to bring New England morals to the peoples of Missouri and then Illinois. Meeting with strong anti-abolitionist sentiments in Missouri, he crossed the Mississippi to Alton, Illinois hoping to find a less virulent atmosphere. This was not to be.

The citizens of Alton persecuted the freedom of the press in much the same way as the citizens of Missouri. Three times, Lovejoy's printing presses were destroyed and thrown into the Mississippi by Alton mobocracy. Determined to guard his new press, Lovejoy had it delivered by river boat under the cover of darkness to a sturdy, stone-walled warehouse on the outskirts of town. He and several like-minded stalwarts set an armed guard about the press to ensure the voice of liberty would continue to be heard in Illinois.

That evening, a mob began gathering in the local taverns, plotting the demise of Lovejoy's press. Around 10 o'clock, the mob commenced to the warehouse, heavily armed and determined to smash the press. Lovejoy and his fellows refused to hand over the press. Members of the mob prepared torches to light the roof of the building on fire. Lovejoy stepped out to dissuade them from burning the building. As he stepped onto the street, shots were fired, striking him in the chest. He cried out, "My God, I am hit!" Stumbling back inside, he died a martyr to the cause.

The perpetrators of the murder are said to have calmly and coldly walked by Lovejoy's body to methodically dismantle the printing press. The press was smashed to pieces and thrown into the Mississippi River, joining the remnants of Lovejoy's three previous presses destroyed by mobs.

Is there no clearer example of the treachery of those who will deny the Constitution of this republic to defend the existence of slavery? The freedoms guaranteed by that document have been smashed as surely as Lovejoy's press. Those who defend the enslavement of the black man now have added to their sins the senseless murder of a white man whose only crime was speaking his conscience. Let the mob beware. Lovejoy's martyrdom will light the spirit fire of every abolitionist, and that fire is sure to sweep across this great land in a conflagration whose only aim will be the complete and immediate abolition of all slavery.

The Last Speech of the Martyr

Reverend Elijah P. Lovejoy's Final Speech to the Citizens of Alton, Illinois delivered on November 3, 1837

"Mr. Chairman, it is not true, as has been charged upon me, that I hold in contempt the feelings and sentiments of this community in reference to the question which is now agitating it. I respect and appreciate the feelings and opinions of my fellow citizens, and it is one of the most painful and unpleasant duties of my life that I am called upon to act in opposition to them. If you suppose, sir, that I have published sentiments contrary to those generally held in this community because I delighted in differing from them or in occasioning a disturbance, you have entirely misapprehended me. But, sir, while I value the good opinion of my fellow citizens, as highly as anyone, I may be permitted to say that I am governed by higher considerations than either the favor or the fear of man. I am impelled to the course I have taken because I fear God. As I shall answer it to my God in the great day, I dare not abandon my sentiments or cease in all proper ways to propagate them.

I, Mr. Chairman, have not desired or asked any *compromise*. I have asked for nothing but to be protected in my rights as a citizen—rights which God has given me, and which are guaranteed me by the constitution of my country. Have I, sir, been guilty of any infraction of the laws? Whose good name have I injured? When and where have I published anything injurious to the reputation of Alton? Have I not, on the other hand, labored, in common, with the rest of my fellow citizens, to promote the reputation and interests of this city? What, sir, I ask, has been my offence? Put your finger upon it, define it, and I stand ready to answer for it.

If I have committed any crime, you can easily convict me. You have public sentiment in your favor. You have your juries, and you have your attorney, and I have no doubt you can convict me. But if I have been guilty of no violation of law, why am I hunted up and down continually like a partridge upon the mountains? Why am I threatened with the tar barrel? Why am I waylaid every day, and from night to night, and my life in jeopardy every hour?

Your have, sir, made up, as the lawyers say, a false issue; there are not two parties between whom there can be a *compromise*. I plant myself, sir, down on my unquestionable rights, and the question to be decided is whether I shall be protected in the exercise and enjoyment of those rights—*that is the question, sir;* whether my property shall be protected, whether I shall be suffered to go home to my family at night without being assailed and threatened with tar and feathers and assassination; whether my afflicted wife, whose life has been in jeopardy from continued alarm and excitement, shall night after night be driven from a sick bed into the garret to save her life from the brickbats and violence of the mobs—*that, sir, is the question.*"

Here, much affected and overcome by his feelings, he burst into tears.

"Forgive me, sir, that I have thus betrayed my weakness. It was the allusion to my family that overcame my feelings. Not, sir, I assure you, from any fears on my part. I have no personal fears. Not that I feel able to contest the matter with the whole community—I know perfectly well I am not. I know, sir, that you can tar and feather me, hang me up, or put me into the Mississippi, without the least difficulty. But what then? Where shall I go? I have been made to feel that if I am not safe at Alton, I shall not be safe anywhere.

I recently visited St. Charles to bring home my family and was torn from their frantic embrace by a mob. I have been beset night and day at Alton. And now if I leave here and go elsewhere, violence may overtake me in my retreat, and I have no more claim upon the protection of any other community than I have upon this, and I have concluded, after consultation with my friends and earnestly seeking counsel of God, to remain at Alton, and here to insist on protection in the exercise of my rights. If the civil authorities refuse to protect me, I must look to God; and if I die, I have determined to make my grave in Alton.

Bridgton, Maine

April 1838

Owen Powers stood at the front of the schoolhouse, drawn to his full height, and looking solemn in his black suit. Clearing his throat, he announced, "Gentlemen, let us begin!" As the citizens of Bridgton took their seats on the school benches, Powers glanced at Parson Joe Fessenden. Parson Joe nodded to him and signaled for him to continue. "We are gathered here tonight to vote on approval of the Constitution of the Bridgton Anti-Slavery Society. Based on our past discussions, I believe we are ready to vote. Reading here from the proposed Constitution:

Article 1st. This Society shall be called the Bridgton Anti-Slavery Society.

Article 2nd. The object of this Society shall be to collect and disseminate correct information of the character of slavery, of the actual condition of the slaves, and free people of color in this country; to endeavor by all laudable means, sanctioned by law, humanity, and religion, to effect the immediate abolition of Slavery in the United States; and to improve and elevate the character and condition of our free colored population.

"May we have a motion to accept this proposed Constitution?"

"Move to accept," came the voice of the Parson.

"Second," sounded out Charles Soule from North Bridgton.

Powers said, "All in favor, say aye." A chorus of ayes rang out strongly. "All agin it, say nay." Silence enveloped the room. "The motion carries. Congratulations, gentlemen, we have a Constitution and may proceed with our mission. Let us begin by asking for guidance from God. Holy God, we thank you for this great crowd of witnesses you have gathered here tonight to work toward freedom for all your children…"

The school room door crashed open, and the room was swamped by the presence of twenty-five or more men bleating, shouting, and leaping about in mockery of a Jim Crow dance. Faces smudged black with charcoal did little to hide the identity of the town's most vocal pro-slavery advocates—Fairbrother, Dennet, Ingalls, and the instigator of the melee, Nat Littlefield. Littlefield shouted, "Disband this meeting, or we will tear this school house down!" The group caused such a fracas that the Anti-Slavery meeting quickly disbanded, heading to Dr. Pease's office to continue discussions after posting a burly doorkeeper to prevent further disturbance. At the conclusion of the meeting, the neighbors nervously left in small groups with the South, Central, and North Bridgton residents traveling together for safety to their respective locales.

The South Bridgton contingent went by wagon and carriage that traveled through Sandy Creek and up over Choate's Hill with only the weak glow of their lanterns to guide their way. George Fitch spoke to Parson Joe as he made to turn into his dooryard, "Be sure to lock up tight tonight, Parson. I don't think we've heard the last of it from those reprobates."

"Will do," replied the Parson. "Watch close on Ingalls Road. God bless you, my friend." The parson drove his horse and carriage into the barn. Unhitching the carriage, he set about making the horse comfortable for the night. He murmured to her quietly as he brushed her down and fetched her grain. Working quickly and efficiently, he soon had all in order. Then, he willed a cheerful smile to his face and headed into the house.

Phebe glanced up from where she sat with her needlework by

the fire. Their adopted niece, Mary Frizzell ran to him, shouting "Uncle!" and threw her arms around him. Phebe rose with her little namesake, Phebe, in her arms and waited for their spirited niece to finish chattering, then she placed a hand on Joe's arm. He leaned down and kissed her cheek, and she looked up into his eyes with unspoken concern. He nodded that all was well.

When the girls were put to bed, Joe sat down with Phebe next to the fireplace. Speaking softly so as not to alarm the girls, Joe said, "We had a bit of trouble tonight." He quickly related the details.

"Oh, Joe, do you think there will be more trouble?"

"It's possible, but I think they've gotten it out of their blood for now. I do not think we need worry," Joe told her.

"I don't know if I'll be able to sleep a wink tonight," Phebe responded with a catch in her voice. "Remember what they did to Reverend Lovejoy? I can't bear to think of you being harmed."

Joe rose from his chair, and reaching for Phebe's hands, he pulled her from her chair and wrapped his arms around her, pulling her close, comforting her. "We are on the side of God and the angels," he told her.

She replied, "So was Lovejoy."

After a restless night, Joe and Phebe went about their morning chores bleary-eyed. Phebe jumped at every noise, and her hand was unsteady on her teacup. Just after 9 o'clock, George Fitch's wagon rolled into the yard, with Washington Chaplin and Daniel Barnard not far behind. Fitch jumped out of his wagon, breathless, and rushed to the kitchen door. Parson Joe opened the door for his friend, asking "What news!?"

Fitch exclaimed, "Parson, you got to hitch your wagon and get out of here. Littlefield and his boys are heading out here. They say they're going to tar and feather you! You need to leave now!"

"Now, slow down, George! Is this confirmed, or is it a rumor?"

"It's confirmed. I was coming back from the Center, and I saw them gathering. They've got the tar and were just fetching the feathers. Littlefield was directing them. I ran the horse as fast as he'd go. We've got to get you somewhere safe!"

"George, you and the other men go on home. I won't be driven out of my house by the likes of Littlefield and his cronies. I won't have them saying they ran me off with their antics."

"Parson, you can't stay! They're on their way now."

Leander Frost came from next door after hearing the ruckus. "Parson, if you're staying, I'll stand by you," he said.

George Fitch said, "Parson, you're sure you shouldn't light out of here?"

Parson Joe shook his head. "I have to trust in the Lord on this."

Fitch replied, "Then, I'm standing next to you." Chaplin and Barnard muttered in agreement.

Joe turned to Phebe who stood with a frightened look on her face, uncertain of what to do. Joe must stand on his convictions, but she wished he would go for his own protection. He spoke firmly to her, "Take the girls into the back house. Stay calm. Trust in God." He looked at Leander and asked, "Leander, will you make sure no harm befalls them?" Leander replied, "Parson, you know you don't even have to ask that. I'll protect them with my life if need be."

The parson and his three bodyguards went into the front hallway, awaiting the arrival of the mob. They heard the mob from down by the cemetery as the wagons and carriages rolled down the road toward the Fessendens' house. "May God bless you and keep you," the parson said to his stalwart friends.

The mob arrived amidst cursing and raucous laughter. "We'll see how the parson likes having black skin," said Ingalls.

"Yeah," replied Dennett, "I'll get the fire going to boil the tar." The rest of the mob milled around the parson's dooryard, shouting insults and demanding he show himself.

Fitch, Chaplin, and Barnard surrounded Joe inside the house. He reached around them for the door handle, intent on addressing the mob. "Parson! No!" shouted Chaplin.

But Parson Joe Fessenden would not be dissuaded from leaving the relative safety of his house. As he stepped out onto his front doorstep, the mob erupted in catcalls and screams, "Tar and feather, tar and feather, tar and feather," they shouted.

Drawing himself up to full pulpit height, Parson Joe called out for silence. At the sound of his commanding voice, the crowd quieted. With his stern gaze raking the crowd, he began to speak. "Friends and Neighbors," he began, "I'd like to welcome you here to my home. It is my pleasure to see so many of you, having not seen some of you in church for such a long time. My good wife would be at my side to welcome you, too, were she not otherwise engaged at the moment."

Glancing at the crowd, he picked out a man at random, "Ah, friend Albert, how is your good wife feeling? And your new little one, how is he?" Albert shuffled his feet, embarrassed. "And Jacob, I've not seen you since we laid your dear mother to rest. We lost a good woman when she went home to the Lord." One by one,

Joe Fessenden disarmed his enemies with his eloquence and charm, until one by one the mob began to dissipate, the men slinking away, their fire burned out. When the last of the mob was gone, Joe turned to his stalwart friends, saying, "You have done me and my family a great service this day. For that I will always be in your debt." He grasped the hand of each in turn. "Now, gentlemen, if you will excuse me, I must go rescue our friend Leander from the clutches of my womenfolk." With that, the day's excitement was at an end.

That night, after the children were tucked in, Joe went to the kitchen looking for Phebe, who was conspicuously absent. He found her with her back to the room, her arms up to the elbows in dish water. Placing his hands gently on her shoulders, he stood silently waiting. After a moment, she spun around and looked into his eyes with exquisite agony etched across her face. "I thought I would lose you as I lost my father," she said in a voice that scraped its way out of her throat. "I thought I would lose you."

She began to sob and he held her tightly, absorbing the storm, holding her until her tears ran dry. He kissed her gently on the forehead, handing her his handkerchief. He started to step away from her, and she reached out a hand and grasped his shirt sleeve. "Please stay close," she whispered.

"I'm right here, my dear friend," he replied. "I'm not going anywhere."

Later, when she slept at last, Joe fell to his knees beside their bed, and silently poured out his anger at his fellow man as tears rolled down his face, turning it all over to the one who holds all the cares and concerns of men close to his bosom.

Freedom's Light
Portland, Maine

Eyewitness Account of the Trial of the Century! Shocking Testimony from Kidnapped Africans

New London, Connecticut

January 7, 1840

The trial to achieve the vindication of the true victims of the Amistad tragedy began today in New London, Connecticut. This reporter was in the courtroom to hear the shocking details of the capture and imprisonment of the unfortunate Africans who are enmeshed in the vagaries of the American justice system. Kidnapped from their homeland in Mendi, Africa by unscrupulous and dastardly slave catchers, the Africans were then sold to slavers in Havana, Cuba—a direct violation of American, Spanish, and English treaties forbidding such trade.

Placed on a ship bound for America, the Africans, who lived in fear for their mortal lives, took matters into their own hands and sought to escape their captors in the only way they could, by breaking their chains and overpowering the ship's crew. In the initial trial, previously reported, the kidnap victims stood stoically in the courtroom, ebony skin glistening in the August heat, unable to speak to defend themselves and unable to understand the proceedings against them due to language barriers, we can only speculate to the state of their minds and the depths of their terror to find themselves in such dire circumstances: far from home, surrounded by gawking strangers, herded together in a crowded courtroom. The slavers who should rightly stand accused have now been brought to justice, arrested on charges of assault, kidnapping, and false imprisonment.

It is a travesty of American justice to force court proceedings against citizens of a foreign nation who neither speak nor understand the language of the proceedings. The Amistad Committee formed by New York abolitionists, with Lewis Tappan taking the lead, have worked diligently to raise funds to defend, house, and care for the unfortunate Africans. An esteemed member of the group, Professor J. Willard Gibbs, undertook learning enough of their native language to seek out a translator. Standing on the waterfront, he counted to ten in the Mendi language until he found a sailor who spoke the language and could translate the testimony of the Africans.

The natural leader of the kidnapped Africans is called Cinque. He is a fine figure of a man, with a noble bearing and strength of frame. He stands tall and proud with his intelligent eyes roving around the courtroom, trying to understand the proceedings swirling around him. Surely this man must be a chieftain of his people in the land from which he was stolen. Through his interpreter, he recounted the capture of his own person and hundreds more unfortunates, some of them being mere children snatched from the very breast of their mothers.

The kidnap victims were forced on board a Spanish ship and spirited away to Havana, Cuba in direct violation of existing treaties. In Havana, they were given false names to mislead the public to their true nationality, then shipped aboard the Amistad to be sold in the American south. Cinque reported the ship's cook had indicated to the unwilling passengers that upon arrival in American, they would be slaughtered and salted down, becoming meat for the table. Terrified, the Africans plotted escape. Cinque took a file and released the catch pin that held the mutual chains of the all the kidnap victims. Waiting for the light of morning, they armed themselves against their captors and set about fighting for their very lives.

Cinque reported that he spared the lives of Ruiz and Montez in exchange for their services to sail the ship back to Africa. Ruiz and Montez instead tricked their victims, sailing slowly as though to Africa during the daylight hours and at a faster pace back toward America at night. At last, with no provisions or fresh water on board, the Amistad stood off the coast of New York. Several Africans came to shore looking for food and water where they were captured yet again by Lt. Gedney who hoped to profit from the sale of the slaves and cargo.

The greed of all involved has not only stolen the lives of the innocent victims but has enmeshed this country in an international maelstrom, endangering the peace and plenty of American citizens. We can only hope and pray that wise men will step into the fray and release these poor unfortunates from the grip of the authorities who have wrongly imprisoned them.

Denmark, Maine

June 1842

Parson Joseph Fessenden's voice boomed loudly through the small meeting house in Denmark. The faithful sat listening intently to his words condemning slavery. Several of the parishioners were scowling at him. Still, he spoke out plainly as to the evils that kept so many supposed Americans from enjoying the full fruits of liberty. When the service ended, the parson stood at the doors of the church to shake hands with the neighbors in this next town over. Although most were polite to the visiting preacher, Joe could sense the hostility of a group of them. They ignored his outstretched hand and stood clumped together in the churchyard, muttering and casting thunderous glances. Phebe could feel the dissension, and she worried for her safety and for Joe's.

As the crowd thinned, Joe and Phebe entered their carriage for the trip back to South Bridgton. Before they left, a gruff, bearded man broke off from the malcontents. Striding over to the carriage, he glared at Joe. "Parson, Sunday meeting ought to be for preaching the gospel, not talking about slavery," he spat out.

Parson Joe looked at the man and said, "It is the duty of a Christian minister to reprove those who do wrong. When a man holds another man in bondage, it is our Christian duty to reprove that man."

"Well, Parson," he nodded toward the assembled group of men, "That right there is part and parcel of the Denmark militia, and you ought to have fair warning that we won't put up with you preaching anything but the gospel on the Sabbath. If we hear you preaching against slavery again, we're coming to South Bridgton, and we'll blow a cannon ball right through the church. Understand?"

Parson Joe stared down the gaze of the angry man. "You may be sure that I will preach against slavery and all the ills of society every day of my life until every American, black, white, or otherwise, is granted the same rights you and I have." With that, he flicked the reins of his horse and the carriage rolled away.

Phebe looked up at Joe with frightened tears in her eyes. "Oh, Joe, do you think they're serious?"

"I doubt it, my dear. The man stank highly of rum. I think it is the spirits talking, and when they have sobered down some, they will sing a different tune."

Phebe looked shocked. "Rum? On the Sabbath? In church?"

"I'm afraid so. Perhaps next time I preach here, I will preach on the dangers of an intemperate life."

Luray, Virginia

July 1842

Mathilde looked up from her corn husk doll when she heard the sound of the cabin door opening. At five, she was a strong child, well formed, with startling blue eyes looking out from a warm brown face. She looked up to see blue eyes like her own in a white man's face. She scrambled quickly to her feet and scampered out of the open cabin door. When Massa come to see her Mama, she was to go outside to play. She pulled the door tight behind her and sat on the stoop drawing pictures in the dirt with a stick. Inside the cabin, she heard the now familiar sounds of Massa grunting and groaning like he always did when he come to see Mama.

After a few minutes, Massa left, patting her fondly on the head as he went by. "You be a good girl, now, Mathilde. Mind you do as you're told." he said. Mathilde skipped back inside. Mama always had a hard look on her face after Massa came. Mathilde wished he wouldn't come any more; it made her Mama sad somehow.

Freedom's Light

Portland, Maine

Amazing Testimony of Escaped Slave Delivered from the Steps of City Hall

September 1842

Speaking extempore from the steps of Portland's City Hall, escaped slave Frederick Douglass shared the story of his shocking treatment at the hands of Southern slaveholders. Douglass spoke eloquently and intelligently to a crowd of a thousand of Portland's citizens and visitors. He well laid aside any doubts as to the intelligence of his race with his eloquent recounting of his years as a slave. The crowd listened raptly to his account, an excerpt of which is here related for the edification of all who could not be in attendance:

Here, too, the slaves of all the other farms received their monthly allowance of food and their yearly clothing. The men and women slaves received as their monthly allowance of food eight pounds of pork, or its equivalent in fish, and one bushel of corn meal. Their yearly clothing consisted of two coarse linen shirts, one pair of linen trousers like the shirts, one jacket, one pair of trousers for winter, made of coarse negro cloth, one pair of stockings, and one pair of shoes—the whole of which could not have cost more than seven dollars.

The allowance of the slave children was given to their mothers, or the old women having the care of them. The children unable to work in the field had neither shoes, stockings, jackets, nor trousers, given to them—their clothing consisted of two coarse linen shirts per year. When these failed them, they went naked until the next allowance day. Children from seven to ten years old, of both sexes, almost naked, might be seen at all seasons of the year.

There were no beds given the slaves, unless one coarse blanket be considered such, and none but the men and women had these. This, however, is not considered a very great privation. They find less difficulty from the want of beds, than from the want of time to sleep, for when their day's work in the field is done, the most of them having their washing, mending, and cooking to do, and having few or none of the ordinary facilities for doing any of these, very many of their sleeping hours are consumed in preparing for the field the coming day; and when this is done, old and young, male and female, married and single, drop down side by side, on one common bed—the cold, damp floor—each covering himself or herself with their miserable blankets; and here they sleep till they are summoned to the field by the driver's horn.

At the sound of this, all must rise, and be off to the field. There must be no halting—every one must be at his or her post, and woe betides them who hear not this morning summons to the field, for if they are not awakened by the sense of hearing, they are by the sense of feeling. Neither age nor sex finds any favour. Mr. Severe, the overseer, used to stand by the door of the quarter, armed with a large hickory stick and heavy cowskin, ready to whip anyone who was so unfortunate as not to hear or, from any other cause, was prevented from being ready to start for the field at the sound of the horn.

Mr. Severe was rightly named—he was a cruel man. I have seen him whip a woman, causing the blood to run half an hour at the time—and this, too, in the midst of her crying children, pleading for their mother's release. He seemed to take pleasure in manifesting his fiendish barbarity. Added to his cruelty, he was a profane swearer. It was enough to chill the blood and stiffen the hair of an ordinary man to hear him talk. Scarce a sentence escaped him but that was commenced or concluded by some horrid oath.

The field was the place to witness his cruelty and profanity. His presence made it both the field of blood and of blasphemy. From the rising 'til the going down of the sun, he was cursing, raving, cutting, and slashing among the slaves of the field, in the most frightful manner. His career was short. He died very soon after I went to Colonel Lloyd's, and he died as he lived, uttering, with his dying groans, bitter curses and horrid oaths. His death was regarded by the slaves as the result of a merciful providence.

South Bridgton, Maine

September 1844

The parson's buggy bounced to a stop in front of his tidy cottage. He reached back to grab his black overcoat just as his wife flung open the kitchen door.

"Joseph," she cried, "They've taken her! They've taken Little Phebe."

"When?" he demanded tensely.

"Just now," she sobbed. "I went to the pantry for preserves to send home with them, and they took off in the carriage. They took her, Joseph. They took our girl." She fell to the doorstep, hands over her face weeping brokenly.

"Listen," he said insistently, "You must listen to me. Go to Leander's. Tell him what's happened. Tell him to follow me as quickly as he can. We'll get her back. We'll get her back." With that, the parson slapped the reins and the buggy lurched forward.

***

The young woman in the carriage glanced nervously over her shoulder. "Do you think they're following?"

"Not yet, Sarah. We've got time. We'll be fine."

The young girl riding between them in the carriage looked up with wide, wondering eyes. Sensing the woman's distress, the girl's brown eyes filled with tears. The woman held her close saying, "It's alright, Phebe, dear. Mama is here. You're going home to live with Mama and Grandpapa, now."

"I want to stay with Uncle," the girl cried as the tears spilled over. "I don't want to go with you!"

***

As the parson's buggy tore up Minister's Hill, the commotion was heard above the hammering in the blacksmith's shop. Leander Frost stuck his head out of the window as the parson flew up the hill. He shouted, "What's wrong, Parson?"

"They've taken our Phebe," the parson shouted.

Not far behind the buggy was the parson's wife, breathless and tear-stained, struggling in her heavy gown. "Leander," she gasped, "Sarah and her father have taken Phebe. Joseph needs your help."

As Leander saddled his horse, he said kindly "We'll get her back, don't worry. Go inside, and the missus will fix you a cool drink." With that, he threw himself in the saddle and headed up the hill in fast pursuit.

***

"Can't we go faster, Father?" Sarah begged.

"The horse is already spent from the trip over, Sarah. I'm doing the best I can."

"Please. I can't let them take my baby again."

Mr. Washburn used the whip to urge the horse on. As they rounded a corner heading uphill, the carriage lurched over a stone in the road. The weary horse overcorrected and the carriage slid wildly sideways heading for a small ravine. Sarah shrieked as the carriage overturned tossing her and the child to the side of the road.

The sounds of Phebe's heart-wrenching screams greeted

Parson Joe as he rounded the turn. Leaping from his buggy, he raced to the over-turned carriage. Mr. Washburn was working to free the horse. Sarah was sitting on the side of the road, scratched and bleeding. Phebe had a growing bump on the back of her head where she had made contact with a rock after being thrown.

When Phebe saw her beloved uncle, she held her arms out to him, sobbing. He picked the child up and spoke soothingly to her as he cradled her head with a gentle hand. The look he gave Sarah and her father was thunderous.

Leander Frost galloped up and swung down from his horse. He ran to help release the horse. He led the horse to a nearby tree and tied her in the shade. When he saw the angry look on the parson's face, he went to him and held out his strong arms to Phebe.

"Come see your old friend, Little One." He spoke to her gently as though she was a frightened horse. She clung to Uncle for a moment until Leander's blue eyes started to twinkle, and he whispered in her ear, "I've got a little something sweet here in my shirt pocket." Letting go her tight hold of Uncle's neck, Phebe leaned toward Leander and found herself warmly cuddled to the big man's chest.

As Leander walked away under the premise of showing Phebe some "pretties," as she called flowers when she was a tiny child, an angry storm broke behind them. The parson rose to full pulpit height and began berating Washburn and Sarah Beach for their carelessness with his young ward.

Sarah started to sob, "I just want my baby with me."

Parson Joe raised his finger and pointed at them both. "That child is the same child you abandoned on our very doorstep, hungry and neglected. And now you dare take her from the only home she's known for nearly ten years. You take her from your sister-in-law who loves her as though she was her own. Washburn, your house is no fit place for this child. Her own father gave me custody of her for that very reason. Sarah, you know you're always welcome to come live with us to be with Phebe. Samuel insists that the child should be raised in the country away from the evil influences of your family. This child belongs with those who can care for her."

Sarah wept. "I love her," she sobbed.

"Then come and live with us. We welcome you with open arms. You know that, girl."

Sarah looked pleadingly at her father who glared at the parson. "Come on, Sarah, let's go. We'll take this matter up in court." Sarah glanced back to where Leander stood holding Phebe. She looked at Parson Joe, her face showed a mixture of regret and defiance, she turned on her heel and climbed into the carriage without the child.

Joseph P. Fessenden to Mr. Carter

South Bridgton

September 30, 1844

Dear Sir,

A kind providence has thus far shielded me and my family amid the tumults and threatenings with which we have been surrounded, and though we all suffered, we are alive this morning and can rejoice in the preserving goodness of God. I send you two dollars, all the money I can now spare as a compensation in part, for your faithful labours in our behalf during the exciting scenes of

Friday and Saturday last. For the kindness and sympathy shown us, I can never compensate you and other friends. All I can do is to thank you most sincerely.

I have not a doubt on looking the whole affair over that the fixed determination of Washburn and his sister Ball engaged with them was to carry at all hazards my darling little ward to Boston. The mother would have regretted the rash act. But she was a passive instrument in the hands of her brother and sister. And but, as I believe, for the timely precautions of Saturday morning, the diabolical deed would have been attempted, if not accomplished. And yourself and my friends, under God, have probably been the means of saving perhaps the life of a darling child and me and my wife from inexpressible agony and distress.

I know better than any around me can the vileness, bitterness, and total want of principle of the Washburn family. And now permit me to say, though I am sure I bear no settled ill will against him, I think you are deceived in reference to the motives which have activated Doctor C. as to the part he has taken in this affair. Not that I have ever given him the least occasion to have any personal dislike to me as a man, but he is a bitter sectarian and has long wished my removal, thinking that my influence stood in the way of the progress in this region of his favourite Methodism. And I believe I do not slander him in saying he has done everything in his power for years to effect my removal.

The affair of my little child is the only occasion he could have to find fault with me and excite a prejudice against me. He has made the best use of it he possibly can. I think I can prove that he has repeatedly said Phebe would not stay long with me but would and should be restored to her mother. I mention these things merely that you may be apprised of what I deem the facts in this case. I cannot leave my family to go to town meeting today. I hope on your return from court you will not fail to call down and see us.

Our united regards to Mrs. Carter and our sincere thanks to you.

Truly yours,

J. P. Fessenden

Joseph P. Fessenden to Doctor John Ware

South Bridgton, Maine

October 28, 1844

Dear Sir,

I write to you to give you background as to why I refused to deliver my ward to Boston as demanded by the mother's family. I believe you will see from the facts herein that I had an ironclad case for doing so.

The mother's first visit was after a lapse of more than two years and lasted a few hours only. The second was after an absence of four years for a stretch of six weeks during which time the child slept with the mother and visited with her at her pleasure. The third visit was eight months after that when the child, in my absence, was seized by a relative of the mother in company with her and dragged from my door and carried to Boston. Where a few weeks after, attended with great anxiety and not a little expense, I made an appeal to one of your judges in your own city, and he decided that the child was rightfully under my care, and I was morally as well as legally bound to protect and support her, and he then delivered her into my hands.

My brother, who assisted me on this occasion, publicly stated in my behalf that notwithstanding all which had happened, the mother could still have free access to her child at my house, see her as often and remain with her as long as she pleased, if she would only be practical and give me no more trouble. The fourth and last visit was the other day in company with her brother, Henry Washburn and sister, Mrs. Ball.

Instead of coming directly to my dwelling, they stopped in an adjoining town at the house of a personal stranger to Mrs. Beach and a bitter sectarian enemy to myself and parishioners. The next day after their arrival, this man called on me with four of my neighbours and informed me that Mrs. Beach, with her brother and sister, was at his house, and the mother wished me to give up the child to accompany her to Boston. If I would not consent to this, she requested that the child might be permitted to be with her a few days while she remained in that neighbourhood. I replied the child will not consent at any rate to go to Boston, neither can I consent to let her go. But I should be glad to have the mother with her child at my house or at the houses of any of the four gentleman present, where she is well acquainted and every accommodation can be afforded her at her own option, not only for a few days but during her life, and I will cheerfully defray all the expenses that may occur on her account. With this offer from me to Mrs. Beach, the man left me.

That night, runners, I know not how many, were sent into four neighbouring towns, carrying the most audacious falsehoods that could be invented, and they made out the next forenoon to collect a gang in sight of my house to the number perhaps of 75, some from state's prison memory, many of drunken notoriety, and not more than five of whom have the pecuniary ability sufficient to pay the fine imposed by our statutes for misdemeanors of the character of which they were guilty. In the rear of this company was Henry Washburn!! Who declared repeatedly to several of my friends as they will confirm under oath that neither he nor his family "cared a fig for the child, nor did they want her!"

At the head of the mob was the man whose house Mrs. Beach had stopped at. He called and informed me, "She was taken suddenly ill, probably would not live the day out, and at any rate could never leave his house alive, and therefore could not come to fulfill either of the plans which I had proposed, and wanted very much to see her child before death!" Under those circumstances, after receiving a guarantee of her safe return to me, the terrified child, in company with two of my friends, visited her mother. And suffice it to say, the mother assured the child, "She did not wish her to go to Boston against her own free consent and directed her to return and live with me."

I saw the mother myself and proposed to her to pass the remainder of her days at my house with her child, and I would do everything in my power for her accommodation and comfort. Now, Sir, since Mrs. Beach by no means wishes me to "constrain" her child to go to Boston (which I should be obliged to do if she went), you will perceive at once that you urge me in your letter not only to the performance of a most painful task but also of a work all together supererogatory. But if it were otherwise, I solemnly assure you, Doctor Ware, I should hesitate very much before I compelled my little ward, to take up her residence, for six months, or I know not how long in a family openly hostile to her guardians, to whom alone in future under God, she can look for protection and guidance and support; to a family, I say, who would not hesitate to use all the efforts in their power to embitter, if possible, her feelings against us. The mother being unable, if disposed, to prevent it, and they have repeatedly proved themselves to be not only reckless of civil law but, as it appears to me, however it may seem to others, reckless also of the decencies of civilized society, I fear not any reproaches hereafter from the child, for not "constraining" her under these circumstances to go to Boston.

Respectfully yours, Reverend Joseph P. Fessenden

Joseph P. Fessenden to prosecuting attorney

South Bridgton

May 7th, 1845

My dear sir,

In a letter recently received from my nephew, W.G. Barrows, I learn you would like as prosecuting officer, to hear from me, in writing, a brief history of my connection with the child and her mother, on whose account, ostensibly, the riotous gathering was excited against me last September, and for which a number of individuals stand indicted and await their trial at the ensuing term of the circuit court in this county. It seems to me very important, in order to have justice done (and this is what and all I am anxious for) that you should know this history, and I will proceed to give it with as much clearness and exactness as I can.

Mr. Beach, the father of this child, is the oldest brother of my wife. He was left fatherless in early life and came to my house when 17 or 18 years old, at Kennebunkport, and made it his home for several years. He went to sea for a livelihood, making a number of voyages first from that port, and afterward sailing from Boston. He was an ardent, generous, and daring fellow, and though soon imbibing many of the characteristics of a sailor of those days, I always found him honest, frank, truthful, and kind.

When mate of a vessel, he became acquainted with a Mr. Ball of the custom house department, who was married to a daughter of James Washburn of Boston, and by Ball, Beach was introduced to the Washburn family as a boarder. When in port, with this family he boarded a number of years and finally married Sarah, one of the daughters, the mother of my ward. All I knew of the family, previous to his marriage was what I learned from a younger brother, who came from Vermont in feeble health for the benefit of the sea air, and who made a visit of three weeks to Mr. Beach, then in port, and boarded with him at Mr. Washburn's.

This younger brother told my wife on his return to our house he feared Samuel was in an improper place, for the family where he boarded made a free use of brandy, and he thought the appearance and conduct of some of the girls exceedingly rude and objectionable. (I afterwards learned from Mr. Beach and his wife and others that Mr. Washburn was habitually intemperate, and that, as a natural consequence, the man was dreadfully profane, quarreled with his wife, and the family was poor.) The two sons being then young, disregarding entirely the Sabbath, and seldom any of them visited a place of public worship.

I have uniformly, when called upon to say any thing on the subject, vindicated the morality of my course in refusing to let the little girl live in Boston with the mother, on the grounds that her father's family, where she was obstinately determined on residing, was an improper place in which to have any child brought up. The legality of my refusal I know could not be questioned for the father of the child constituted to me by written indentures the guardianship of the child, and more over, solemnly enjoined it upon me to keep the child under my own roof, in my own family. And it has always appeared to me and still does appear, that every judicious man and woman, father and mother, in this community must perceive at once that I should have acted a most unfaithful and wicked part both in service to Mr. Beach and the little girl had I suffered the mother to carry her into a great city like Boston, and bring her up in a family, the head of which I knew was intemperate, profane, and quarrelsome, and some of the female members possessing characteristics, I had been led to believe, at least rather suspicious and questionable.

After Mr. Beach was married and the child in question was born, he wrote us from Boston, making earnest request that we would board for a fair compensation his wife and child for some few years, while he went to sea, that it would be greatly for his interest in a pecuniary point of view, but the considerations that especially induced him to make the request was as his wife was young and her education had been entirely neglected, he was sure it would be for her advantage, mentally, morally, and domestically to reside some time in our family. We wrote him in reply that as his wife had always lived in a city, we feared she could not be contented and thus her situation and our own would be rendered very unpleasant. We, therefore, should decline to take her as our boarder, but we invited her to make us a visit of three months in his absence, and we would endeavour to do all in our power for her comfort and happiness.

He wrote again, saying he was anxious to have his wife and child under our care, and we finally consented to take them, fixing the compensation at a dollar per week. Accordingly, in October 1835, he brought them to our house. The child then being not quite three months old. They resided with our family together about two years. I received of his money for their board, two years, ninety dollars. And let me here say, this is all the pecuniary compensation I have ever received or ever expect to receive, for the support and education of the child and all the expense and troubles I have been put to on her account. I mention this merely because busy bodies have for years been industriously circulating the falsehood and probably sending it to the ears of the Washburn family that I have all along been receiving large remittance from Mr. Beach, and this is the reason why I have held on to the child with such unyielding pertinacity.

We learned from Mr. Beach when he brought his wife and child to our house that Mr. Washburn was habitually intemperate, awfully profane, and often quarreled with this wife and that as a natural consequence, the family was poor and irreligious. Two sons-in-law with their wives and children resided then under the same roof with Mr. Washburn, one of whom was a professed disciple of Abner Kneeland, that freethinking evangelist of the Universalist church, prosecuted for blasphemy in Massachusetts.

He moreover assured us that if his wife remained with her father, all the money he left in her hands for her benefit would go for the support of the family, of which no amount would be rendered to her, that during one short voyage of three months, a hundred dollars of his hard earnings had been thus disposed of and that, before marriage, he made an explicit agreement with his wife that she was not to live in Boston in his absences at sea, but in some suitable place in the country which he would provide for her. He also told us the agreement was that no child or children of his were to be brought up there unless he was with them as a protector.

Besides, we gathered from repeated conversations had with Mrs. Beach during her stay with us that the above statements of Mr. Beach respecting her father and his family were correct, and that the arrangement he made for her residence with her child in the country was both judicious and necessary. Upon the above incontestable facts, brought to my knowledge by Mr. and Mrs. Beach and others, I have rested the vindication of the morality of my course, in refusing to let the little girl live with her mother in Boston.

When arraigned before the bar of envious and meddlesome people around me, who have endeavoured at all counts to try and pass sentence upon my conduct and condemn me, I have had other reasons but have mentioned them only in a very few instances to particular friends as I supposed and am still reluctant on the absent father's and the child's account, as well as on account of the memory of the deceased mother, unless absolutely necessary in self-vindication. But these reasons I will name to you.

I was suspicious from the statement made to my wife by the brother of Mr. Beach, already alluded to from the anxiety of Mr. Beach to have his wife under our care and his absolute refusal to let her visit Boston, should she be discontented, during his absence at sea, that some of the females of the Washburn family and perhaps Mrs. Beach herself, might be of loose morality in respect to chastity. Accordingly, when he finally separated from his wife and went to Florida, she positively and absolutely did go astray of her morals.

The mother, Sarah, did die recently in Boston of consumption. My enemies reported that she died of missing her child. Some of my neighbours turned against me and caused a mob to form at my home, frightening my wife and my wards, including the child in question. The mother left the child with us when she was but two years old and did not return until the child was four, at which time the mother and her father, James Washburn did steal the child from the safety of her home. The mother did not come to see the child again until she was eight years of age.

When the child was four, the mother and her relatives sued for custody, taking the child away to Boston. The court determined, based on evidence and the testimony of the child's own father, that she was clearly my ward and was to remain in the only home she has ever known.

The mother died of consumption in Boston and the father, Samuel Beach was sailing out of Savannah, Georgia. He has ever intended and has instructed me always directly to prevent at any cost the child living with her mother's family in Boston. To preserve the honour of the mother and therefore the child, I have withheld details of the mother's moral character and as such have been the victim of recriminations from some of the leading citizens of this town who, ignorant of the details, have accused me of breaking the natural bond between mother and child.

The mob that came to my house was made up mostly of hard drinkers of rum who were far more troubled by my stance against strong spirits than by any concern for my child.

Another mob formed in Naples and hanged up a straw man in the village said to represent me. They poured rum on it and lit it on fire. This caused my wife great distress. I have ever tried to do what is best and right for all involved in this sad case. I continue to do as the father of the child has always wished me to do.

Respectfully,

Joseph P. Fessenden

Freedom's Light
February 1849

Thrilling Escape from Slavery!

We have received news of the thrilling escape of two slaves, husband and wife. They slipped their bonds by an act of sheer bravery and determination. Traveling from Georgia to Boston by means of clever disguise, Ellen and William Craft now join the ranks of escaped slaves speaking on the abolitionist circuit. We share with you the following letter printed in our sister newspaper *The Liberator*:

Pineville, Pennsylvania

Jan. 4, 1849.

DEAR FRIEND GARRISON:

One of the most interesting cases of the escape of fugitives from American slavery that have ever come before the American people has just occurred under the following circumstances: William and Ellen Craft, man and wife, lived with different masters in the State of Georgia. Ellen is so near white that she can pass without suspicion for a white woman. Her husband is much darker. He is a mechanic, and by working nights and Sundays, he laid up money enough to bring himself and his wife out of slavery. Their plan was without precedent and, though novel, was the means of getting them their freedom.

Ellen dressed in man's clothing and passed as the master, while her husband passed as the servant. In this way, they traveled from Georgia to Philadelphia. They are now out of the reach of the bloodhounds of the South. On their journey, they put up at the best hotels where they stopped. Neither of them can read nor write. And Ellen, knowing that she would be called upon to write her name at the hotels, etc., tied her right hand up as though it was lame, which proved of some service to her, as she was called upon several times at hotels to 'register' her name.

In Charleston, S. C., they put up at the hotel which Gov. McDuffie and John C. Calhoun generally make their home, yet these distinguished advocates of the 'peculiar institution' say that the slaves cannot take care of themselves. They arrived in Philadelphia in four days from the time they started. Their history, especially that of their escape, is replete with interest. They will be at the meeting of the Massachusetts Anti-Slavery Society in Boston in the latter part of this month, where I know the history of their escape will be listened to with great interest. They are very intelligent. They are young, Ellen 22 and William 24 years of age. Ellen is truly a heroine.

Yours, truly,

William Wells Brown

Freedom's Light
March 1849

This Side Up: The Daring Escape of Henry "Box" Brown!

Word has reached us from our brothers at the Philadelphia Anti-Slavery Society office of the daring escape of a Virginia slave. Henry Brown caused himself to be nailed into a wooden crate measuring only two feet wide, three feet long, and two and a half feet deep. With help from friends, who for their protection shall remain unnamed, Brown was shipped from Richmond, Virginia to Philadelphia inside a box about half the size of a coffin. Three holes were drilled in the box to allow Brown to breathe. His only provisions were a small bladder of water and some biscuits. The box was marked "Dry Goods" and "This Side Up," and addressed to the Pennsylvania Anti-Slavery Society.

Alerted to the impending delivery, James Miller McKim, to whom the box was addressed, waited with great trepidation. When the box arrived, after an arduous journey lasting 27 hours and covering a distance of 350 miles under the worst possible circumstances, McKim quickly grasped a crow bar prying open the box. As the lid was pried off, Brown rose to his feet saying, "How do you do, gentlemen?" He immediately then fainted dead away. Under the ministrations of the men at hand, he soon was revived at which time he burst into song, singing:

"I waited patiently; I waited patiently for the Lord, for the Lord; And he inclined unto me, and heard my calling; I waited patiently; I waited patiently for the Lord."

What would drive a man to seek freedom at such great peril? Brown reported to McKim that he was distraught at the sale of his wife, Nancy, and their children to parts unknown. Having determined life was no longer worth living without his family, Brown enlisted the help of friends to spirit him away under the very noses of his captors and if he should live another day it would be as a free man or not at all.

Freedom's Light
September 18, 1850 Day of Infamy and Despair

Fugitive Slave Act Passes! No Coloured Man or Woman is Safe!

The United States Congress has dealt another death blow to the freedoms guaranteed to all the citizens of this country. This heinous Act overturns State's Rights to enact personal liberty laws to protect coloured citizens. The Act gives sweeping powers to police, judges, and slaveholders.

Law enforcement officials are now required to arrest any persons who are even suspected of being runaway slaves on the mere testimony of a slaveholder. Under the Act, the suspected runaway is given no right to testify on his own behalf and is not granted a jury trial as other citizens are. Anyone aiding an alleged runaway slave is subject to a $1,000 fine and six months imprisonment. Law enforcement officials are entitled to a bounty for the capture of any alleged escaped slaves.

How in this country founded on personal liberty has such a catastrophic Act been voted into law? Many say the blame rests squarely on the shoulders of that traitor to New England, Black Dan'l Webster. His support of the Act is said to have swayed the vote. That a man as New England to the core as Webster is could so turn against the laws and wishes of all of New England speaks to the dissipation of his formerly sterling character. His claim that anyone aiding a fugitive is a traitor to his country shows just how far he has fallen from this own inclinations and reeks of political maneuvering for the Presidency he covets. He shall find no votes in all of New England! And no welcome in any home or at any fireplace!

Mathilde

Pendergast Tobacco Plantation, Luray, Virginia

March 1851

Young Massa slammed Mathilde's thin body against the side of the drying shed as she struggled to escape his grasp. Tearing the thin fabric of her muslin dress, he groped her tender flesh, mauling at her breasts like a demented beast. He pressed his face close to hers, his breath stinking of his father's whiskey. "Stop fighting me if you value your life," he warned. He slapped her hard across the face, bloodying her nose and making her cry out from the pain. He shoved a hard hand across her mouth. "Shut up, you black whore. Shut up or die."

Grabbing her arms, he spun her around crushing her against the shed wall. After fumbling with his pants, she felt his flesh touch hers and shuddered. Within minutes, the attack was over. He released her, and she fell to the ground. He delivered a kick to her midsection. "Tell my father, and I'll make sure you get sold to New Orleans. That's where they send the whores. And that's all you are now, a worthless whore." He left her lying there, her body bloodied and battered, her soul shattered.

Mathilde

Blue Ridge Mountains

March 1851

Mathilde crawled stiffly from the cave where she sheltered from the heat of the day. Brushing off dirt and leaves, she took stock of her surroundings. The Indian trail continued up higher into the mountain landscape, littered with jagged rocks softened by velvety green moss. As she climbed higher, the trees were smaller, stunted by the wind that blew over the high elevations of the Blue Ridge. From the plantation, these mountains seemed small and gentle, shrouded in the blue haze that gave them their name. Climbing those mountains, Mathilde found them to be anything but gentle. Climbing them in the dark was a nightmare. She fell repeatedly, tripping over roots and boulders, bruising her shins and elbows. The sharp rocks scored her feet with scrapes and bruises making walking all the more difficult.

After a night of such struggles with the terrain, the first glimmer of the rising sun showed itself as a sliver of light over the Blue Ridge. She knew she must find shelter soon. A rock outcropping or a small cave or a thicket of brambles. Any place she could hide from the slavers who by now would be searching the woods for her. She thought of her mother and worried if her running would bring trouble to her. She prayed it would not. The thought of her mother brought tears to Mathilde's eyes. She knew in her soul she would never again in this lifetime see her mother's face. She impatiently wiped away her tears, smearing more dirt on her face. She had no time for grief. She had to keep putting one foot in front of the other with each step taking her farther from the plantation and closer to the safety she hoped to find in the North.

She continued to climb, and her breath grew ragged with the exertion. With her hands scrabbling, she pulled herself over the roughest areas. Her gaze swept the landscape, continually looking for a safe haven as the light grew stronger. She must find a place to hide soon before full light. She pulled herself up the final steep slope to the top of the mountain. As she reached the rocky ledge of the summit, she stood silhouetted on the high ground as the sun rose over the neighboring mountain. She gazed out over the panorama of nature's splendor, seeing mountain after mountain and green, rolling valleys for as far as her eyes could see. Her breath caught in her chest as she saw for the first time the wideness of the world. She turned to face the sun and lifting her arms open and wide and letting her head fall back, she let the sun's rays bathe her in light as she breathed in the freshness of the mountain air. For the first time in her young life, she felt truly alive.

A rustling in the underbrush ended the moment for her, and mindful of the danger of standing in the open in the daylight, she frantically searched the landscape for a hiding place. Finding a large outcropping of rocks, she squeezed herself into a small overhang. Curling up like a cat by the fire, she dropped into an exhausted sleep.

The coolness of the late afternoon woke her from a nightmare. She dreamt of bloodhounds hard on her trail, felt their hot breath as they leapt toward her throat. Jerking awake, she lay panting with her hands about her neck protecting it from the teeth of the dogs. She rose with hunger pulling at her belly. It had been two days since she'd eaten. With no house in sight, she knew her only hope of food was to forage for fresh berries or last year's nuts. A search of the area yielded a small handful of seedy raspberries. Stuffing them in her mouth, she began to walk, descending now, down into the next valley. With dusk coming on, she faced another long night of fumbling north through the darkness.

As the darkness deepened, she walked along dejectedly. Far from all that was familiar, adrift in a vast wilderness, and utterly, undeniably alone and without protection. Mathilde gasped aloud as the enormity of her perilous situation settled in to her breast. Had she run from one danger only to die alone in the wilderness? And what death would befall her? Starvation? Wolves? Slavers? Dogs? Snakes? Overcome, she fell to her knees, sobbing. With her face in her hands she cried out against the unpitying harshness of life. She wept for the loss of her mother, for the cruelty of her existence, and the heartbreak of her birth. Her keening cries in the wilderness were that of a mortally-wounded animal.

When at last she had emptied out her heart and laid bare her soul and washed the earth with the salt of her tears, she lay as though dead on the forest floor. A vast nothingness filled her, an echoing void. She waited, spent, hoping death would take her. Into that void, crept a small, whispering voice. "I'm on my way to Canaan land. I'm on my way to Canaan land. Glory hallelujah, I'm on my way." What was that? It was so familiar to her. She cast about in her mind trying to identify it. Mama. This is the song she was always singing. Scraps of the words came slowly back to her. "I'm falling and rising. I'm on my way. I'm falling and rising. Yes, I'm on my way. On my way to Canaan land." The soulful sound of her mother singing to her rose up in her breast. Rising from the ground, she put one foot forward slowly, then the second foot, and as she began to walk, she sang "Had a mighty hard time, but I'm on my way. Had a mighty hard time, but I'm on my way. Had a mighty hard time, but I'm on my way. On my way to Canaan land."

Placing each step carefully, feeling her way through the darkness, Mathilde found her way along the Indian trail through the forest. She was faint from hunger and was watching the sky for the glimmer of dawn when she could hopefully find some berries to eat. At last in the loneliness of the night, she could just make out the tiniest sliver of light on the horizon. As she made her way past a large rock outcropping, she was startled to see a clearing and in that clearing several buildings.

A rooster crowed, startling her. A rooster. A rooster meant hens. Hens meant eggs. Mathilde looked longingly toward the small shack that must hold the chickens. Preacher said stealing was against Jesus. But surely Jesus wouldn't deny her one small egg. Screwing up her courage, she cautiously stepped into the clearing, as shy as a newborn fawn. Walking slowly, keeping low, she approached the chicken coop. Carefully pulling open the door, she stepped quietly inside. The startled hens set up a racket, flying about in a panic. Mathilde grabbed an egg from the nearest nest, and cracking the shell, she gulped down the contents as she rushed out of the coop.

Heading back the way she came at a dead run, she was terrified to hear the sound of a dog barking as it raced toward her, quickly followed by the sound of a door slamming open and a man's voice shouting. As Mathilde lit out over the clearing at a dead run, she felt the dog grab hold of her dress. The worn fabric tore away. Sobbing, she struggled to continue, but the dog lunged again, grabbing her arm and pulling her to the ground. Mathilde curled into a ball, protecting herself from the dog's teeth as best she could.

A man's voice called off the dog and then said, "What in blazes are you doing in my chicken coop?" He thrust the lantern into her tear-stained, scratched, and filthy face. She heard the intake of his breath at the sight of her face. Turning toward the house, he shouted, "Rebecca, come quick!" He leaned down to help Mathilde rise, but she jerked away from him in terror.

Rebecca Stultz ran from the house at her husband's call.

"What is it Jakob?"

"Another runaway," he replied.

Rebecca saw the terror on Mathilde's face and the immodest state of her torn clothing. She turned to her husband and said, "Let me take care of this, now, husband. This is woman's work. Would you stir up the fire and fill the big kettle for me?" Jakob nodded, turning back toward the house with the dog reluctantly at his heels. Rebecca knelt in the dirt and stretched out a hand to the frightened girl. "You are safe, my dear. No harm shall come to you here. What is your name?"

"Mathilde," came the answer.

"Oh, that's a lovely name. Mathilde, are you hungry?" Mathilde nodded her head. "Well, come with me. Come inside, and I'll fix you some breakfast. And we'll get you a different dress to wear. Yours seems to have met some misfortunes in your travels." Mathilde rose slowly from the ground, glancing about fearfully. Rebecca placed a gentle hand on her back to guide her. Mathilde flinched with pain.

Entering the cabin door, Mathilde looked nervously about for the dog. Seeing her concern, Jakob said, "You need not worry about the dog. I left her in the barn with the stock." Seeing the girl's embarrassment at the state of her clothing, he turned to his wife and said, "I'll do the milking and gather the eggs now. I'm sure our guest will want some privacy."

Rebecca threw him a grateful look and gave him a sweet smile. When he left, Rebecca began chattering away, trying to make Mathilde feel more comfortable. "Now, dear, step behind the hanging quilt and get out of that dress. The water should be warm soon, and you can get cleaned up while I start breakfast. Oh, wait! Let me get you a dress to wear. I'm sure one of mine will fit you just fine." She bustled about, laying all in readiness for Mathilde. Then, leaving the girl alone to wash and dress, she set about slicing bacon and fresh bread.

When Mathilde had dressed, she stepped from behind the quilt and said shyly, "Ma'am, this dress buttons up the back."

Rebecca replied, "Oh, let me help you with that." Turning her round, Rebecca began fastening the small buttons. She caught her breath when she saw the bruises on Mathilde's back. Holding her tongue, she gently fastened the rest of the buttons, saying cheerfully, "Well, now, you must feel a sight better getting cleaned up! Let me just call Jakob, and we'll sit down for a good feed."

The sun rose over the Blue Ridge, flooding the cabin with rosy light. Jakob bowed his head, saying, "Father, we ask for your blessing this morning. We thank you for the food you have provided for us. We thank you for bringing a lost lamb into our fold. We ask your help and guidance as to how to best help her to find the life you mean for her to live. Amen."

With a smile, Rebecca heaped food onto the plate of her husband and her unexpected guest. Mathilde looked with wonder at the plenty on her plate. "Eat up, dear," urged Rebecca, "You need your strength." Mathilde reached her hands into her plate and began stuffing food into her mouth. When her plate was empty, Rebecca filled it again until Mathilde could hold no more. "Now, Mathilde, I think you need a good sleep." Rebecca got up from the table, picking up plates as she went. She stepped over to a cedar chest at the foot of the bed, pulling out a brightly colored quilt. She handed it to Mathilde, indicating the ladder to the loft. "Climb right up. You'll be snug as can be up there and no one will know you are here."

Mathilde climbed up the ladder to the loft. She found all to be tidy there, just as down below. From the rafters hung braids of onions and garlic and drying lavender. She found a nook in the back behind a barrel and curled up into a ball, wrapped tightly in the quilt. With a belly full of simple, good cooking, she sighed once and fell into an exhausted sleep.

Mathilde slept through the day and was awoken at dusk by the sounds of Rebecca preparing the evening meal. Stiffly, she rose from the floor, carefully folding the quilt and putting it on top of the barrel. She went to the edge of the loft and swinging her legs over, climbed down the ladder. Rebecca turned to her with a smile, "You look much more rested," she said. "Supper will be ready soon. I hope you like chicken stew and dumplings."

Mathilde nodded her head shyly. Quietly, she said, "You need some help? My Mama taught me how to make dumplings."

Rebecca reached over to the cupboard and handed Mathilde a large bowl. "You'll find everything you need right there on the table." Mathilde set about measuring flour by eye, cutting in the lard, and adding fresh milk. When the dumpling mixture was ready, she dropped spoonfuls into the hot stew, turning them gently as they cooked.

When Jakob came through the door, exhausted from a day in the fields, he kissed his wife on the cheek and said to the women, "My father gave me wise advice. Don't marry a woman who is pretty. Marry a woman who can cook. I was smart enough to get both." Rebecca blushed prettily. Mathilde watched how they were together and saw how a man and a woman could be kind to each other, something she'd never really seen in her life. She tucked away that newfound discovery for another day when she had time to ponder such things.

After enjoying a large bowl of stew and dumplings, Jakob

pushed back his bowl and looked at Mathilde. "We have much to talk about this night," he said. Mathilde looked at him nervously. "You have naught to fear, daughter," he said.

Mathilde

Blue Ridge Mountains

April 1851

Jacob Stultz pushed back his chair and reached for his pipe. As he tamped down the tobacco into the bowl, he looked Mathilde in the eyes. "We haven't asked you where you came from or how you ended up here. From the look of you, my guess is you're on the run." Mathilde leaped from her place at the table, intent on escaping from the cabin.

Rebecca spoke quickly, "You will come to no harm here. You are among friends. We only want to help you find your way to safety." Mathilde's eyes darted back and forth between Jakob and Rebecca trying to read what was happening as she always had on the plantation. Being able to understand quickly which way the wind blew was a slave's best defense against punishment. In the eyes of her hosts, she saw only concern and kindness. Taking a deep breath, she sidled back toward the table.

Jakob began to speak again. "We have some friends who will help you from here all the way up to Canada."

Mathilde asked, "What is Canada?"

Jakob replied, "It's a land up North where there is no slavery."

"No slavery," repeated Mathilde, trying to understand what

that meant.

"No slavery," said Jakob, "Every one is free."

Mathilde looked at him with confusion. How could there be a land where everyone was free? She had heard stories of such a place, but she never believed them to be true. "No fooling?" she asked.

Jakob chuckled, "No fooling. Would you like our help to get there?" She nodded cautiously, still not sure if the white man could be trusted.

Rebecca spoke, saying, "You're not the first runaway to come into our cabin. And if the Lord wills it, you won't be the last."

Jakob nodded as he puffed on his pipe, "We can help you, if you'll let us. We'll give you food and a lantern and send you on to the next station to some friends who will help you on the next leg of the journey. Ma'am, I want you to know this. You're no longer alone. You have brothers and sisters all along the way who will help you get to freedom."

Mathilde's eyes grew wide as what the man was saying began to sink in. After days of being on the run, to imagine someone would help her—a stranger, a slave girl—was more than she could comprehend. "Why you help me?" she asked her voice catching in her throat. "I ain't nobody to you."

Rebecca smiled warmly at her and quoted, "And the King shall answer and say unto them, 'Verily I say unto you, inasmuch as ye have done it unto one of the least of these, my brethren, ye have done it unto me.'"

A look of recognition crossed Mathilde's face. "Preacher said those words at meeting. Said that Jesus talking."

Rebecca smiled, "That's right. We try to live those words every day."

Jakob leaned forward and began to speak, "Sister, do you know the stars they call the drinking gourd? Can you find them in the sky?"

"Sure," replied Mathilde, "My Mama showed me. She told me 'bout the North Star, too. Said it showed the way to Canaan Land."

"Good, good!" said Jakob. "That's the first thing you need to know to travel on. You'll need to keep traveling at night so you can always keep the North Star in sight. But, from now on, you won't travel alone. As soon as dusk falls, I'll hitch the wagon and take you to the next stop on the railroad."

Mathilde said, fearfully, "Never been on a train before."

"Oh, it's not really a train, dear," explained Rebecca. "Just a way of talking in a code so others don't know what we do. Now, let's pack up some food for the trip."

At dusk, Jakob hitched up the wagon and hid Mathilde in the bed under a pile of burlap sacks tucked under a covering of hay. Bidding Rebecca lock the cabin up tight and keep the rifle close, he lightly tapped the reins on the horse's back, and they set off down the crude mountain road. Several hours later, the wagon came to a stop in another clearing. A barking dog caused Mathilde to whimper and curl tightly into a ball in the back of the wagon. Jakob softly called out, "Here, Shep, good dog." The dog came running to the familiar voice of a friend. He leapt about, excited at the presence of a visitor.

The door to the cabin opened, and Jakob whistled softly. The cabin's occupant, used to late night arrivals, spoke softly to someone in the cabin before stepping out and pulling the door closed behind him. Without a word, the man pulled open the barn door as Jakob went to the back of the wagon and called quietly to Mathilde, "Come out quickly, sister. We need you under cover and safe. You're among friends." Mathilde eased herself out of the wagon bed, and the man at the barn door waved her inside. Jakob quickly climbed back into the wagon and, without a word, drove smoothly away.

Mathilde stood in the faint light of the lantern and looked about the barn. The man motioned for her to come with him. He pointed to the loft and softly said, "You'll find a quilt up behind the straw bales. You'll rest here for a day before we move you on to the next station. God bless you, sister. My wife will bring you food in the morning." With that, he left. Mathilde carefully held her lantern as she climbed the ladder to the hay loft. Looking around, she found the quilt. Burrowing under the hay, she made a safe nest and covered herself with the quilt. She blew out the lantern and lay staring into the darkness. As she sank deeper into the hay, and her heart stopped pounding, she could hear the small rustling of mice in the hay and the patient sound of the milk cow chewing her cud. She let the rhythmic sound lull her to sleep.

The sound of horses in the yard woke Mathilde from a deep sleep. Bolting straight upright, the sound of her sharp intake of breath was like the frightened noise of a deer in the pale dawn. Casting her eyes about the hay loft, she desperately looked for a more secure hiding place. Wadding up the quilt that had kept her warm through the night, she frantically burrowed into the loose hay, pulling it quickly over her and scrambling backwards, continuing to burrow as far back as she could go until she felt the wall at her back. She forced herself to control her panicked breathing, detaching her spirit from her body to steady herself. She carefully put the balled up quilt in front of her face to allow some breathing space.

The voices in the yard confirmed her fears. "We're looking for a runaway slave," said a gruff male voice. "We think she might be hiding out in these parts."

She heard the farmer calmly reply, "Ain't seen nobody round here."

"Mind if we look around?" came the reply.

"Look if you want, don't make no difference to me."

Mathilde heard men dismounting horses. Maybe three men. Maybe four. She heard the barn door creak open, and the cow moving restlessly in her stall. Two men moved about in the barn below her hiding place. She heard them talking desultorily about the condition of their crops and the need for rain. Methodically, they worked their way around the small barn. She heard them raise and slam shut the cover of the grain bin. One of them said, "I'll check the loft." He placed one foot then the next as he climbed the ladder. She held her breath, her heart beating madly against her ribs. She heard him moving about, shifting bales of hay as he went. Finding the pile of loose hay, he kicked at the edges with his boot. Then, picking up a pitchfork, he set about jamming it into the loose hay. Mathilde heard the thunk of the pitchfork hitting the barn floor, closer and closer to where she lay. She curled smaller and smaller. The thrusting pitchfork came down from above her puncturing the quilt in front of her face.

From the small cabin came the sound of a frantically crying baby and the angry voice of the baby's mother, "How dare you come in here! How dare you wake this baby! I have been up all night with him, colicky as he is. I just now got him to sleep. You get right out of this cabin now, or I swear I will beat you like your mother should have! The nerve of you busting in here, disturbing peaceable folks with your nonsense. Get out before I take the broom to you."

The man in the hayloft shouted down to his compatriot, "Well, we're in for it now. Angry woman is worse than a scalded cat. Nothing here anyway. We'd best high-tail it 'fore she comes after us like she's doing to Gus right now." With that, he swung himself down the ladder, and the two men beat a hasty retreat. They swung themselves onto their horses and rode quickly away with the steady harangue of an outraged woman echoing behind them out of the clearing.

The farmer kissed his brave wife and his son, and strode to the barn. Calling softly from below, he said, "Ma'am, they're gone. Are you well?"

Mathilde whispered through the floorboards, "They did not find me."

"Stay low. Tonight we will get you to the next station. We'll move you as soon as night falls."

Mathilde

Eastern Pennsylvania

May 1851

How many miles had they bumped along? Mathilde's knees and elbows were bruised and sore from being tossed about in the back of the farmer's wagon. Peeking out from under the tarp, she could see nothing but green landscape that seemed to stretch on forever. This land had a mystical feel to it, as though it was inhabited by small strange beings. Mathilde expected to see a bearded half man-half forest animal peering around the slate rock outcropping. In the distance, she could hear the sound of water rushing over the rocks.

As the sun worked its way across the Pennsylvania sky, Mathilde dozed often, each time woken by the jolting of the wagon on the rough frontier road. When she thought they would drive on like this forever and despair was taking hold of her heart, she heard the sound of a dog barking. Cringing back into the corner of the wagon, she waited for disaster to strike. The wagon rolled to a stop. Fearfully peeking out from her hiding place, Mathilde could see the corner of a building but nothing that helped her to know where she was.

As she lay waiting to see what would happen next, she was startled to see the face of a young boy looking at her from the end of the wagon. Catching her breath, she held as still as she could, not daring to breathe. The boy looked at her with solemn eyes. "Why are you in the wagon?" he asked. Mathilde did not answer for fear he would sound the alarm. The boy pulled himself up into the wagon. "Don't you know how to talk?" he asked. Mathilde continued to stare at him, wordlessly. "My name is Andrew. I'm six years old. How old are you?" Taking no notice of her lack of response, the boy prattled on about his sisters, his dog, and how he caught the fish that his family had for supper the night before.

Mathilde continued to watch him while he rattled on. "ANDREW! Get down from that wagon this instant," came a woman's voice. Mathilde froze. "George, give me a hand please." An unseen hand turned back the tarp, exposing Mathilde to view. Petrified, she lay curled in a ball. The woman's voice came again, gentle now, "Miss, you are safe here. Let me help you down from the wagon." Mathilde turned stiffly onto her hands and knees, crawling to the end of the wagon. The woman took her elbow, helping her to the ground and steadying her as she swayed on her feet. "I'm Mrs. Dennis, and you are welcome here. My husband, George, is the one who drove you here. You must come in by the fire and have a bowl of soup. You'll sleep here tonight until we can arrange for your safe passage."

Glancing up, Mathilde saw the house was sturdy and well-built compared to some of the other houses she had stayed in on the way. Mrs. Dennis motioned Mathilde to a chair at the kitchen table and dished up a bowl of soup. She laid a loaf of fresh bread next to it and invited Mathilde to eat her fill. As Mathilde ate, young Andrew came and leaned his elbows on the table, watching her eat. Mrs. Dennis shook her apron at him, saying, "Scoot! Before I find you something to do." He sat down on the floor in the corner, playing with a crudely made toy boat. He was soon joined by his sisters, Hannah and Kathryn. The three children played quietly for a short while, before growing bored.

Andrew got up and went to his mother, pulling at her skirts. "Can that lady tell us a story?"

His mother replied, "That lady's name is Miss Mathilde, and you must ask her if she has a story she would like to tell you."

Andrew turned his eyes to Mathilde. His sisters rose up and shyly came to stand near him. "Will you?" asked Andrew. "Will you tell us a story?"

Mathilde looked at the hopeful eyes of the three children, and she felt her heart warm toward them. She cast about for a story to tell. Surely she could tell these innocents no stories from her own life. She tried to think of a story but could not, so she shyly said, "I could sing you the song I sing while I'm traveling." Andrew nodded his head and his sisters drew closer. Mathilde took a deep breath began to sing, "I'm on my way to Canaan Land, I'm on my way." She started out nervously at first, then she found herself getting lost in the rhythm of the song, just as she did walking along the mountain trail. With growing confidence, she funneled all the pain and fear and longing into her song. "Had a mighty hard time. But I'm on my way. Had a mighty hard time. But I'm on my way. On my way to Canaan Land."

The sweetness of her voice poured forth the depth of her emotions. When she was done, the children stood looking at her with great round eyes, and Mrs. Dennis had tears running down her face as she sat in the rocking chair by the fire. Silence fell over the room until all that could be heard was the popping of the flames in the fire place and the ticking of the mantle clock.

Mathilde

Boston, Massachusetts

May 1851

The carriage rolled down the crowded streets of Boston. Mathilde looked about her with awe. Never had she seen anything like the sights and sounds of the city. Fashionable carriages like the one she rode in, farm wagons carrying cabbages and string beans, street vendors hawking apples or ribbons or chickens. Tidy storefronts, rundown tenements with laundry hung out to dry, buildings taller than any she'd ever seen. The smells were an overwhelming mixture of raw sewage, rotting animal carcasses, tangy salt air, and sweet spices from the Orient. Mathilde's head swiveled every direction trying to take it all in.

Just to be sitting on the seat of a carriage was an experience. Now that she was truly in the North, she was given the freedom of riding in plain sight for the first time. She looked around at the faces on the street, most white, but many black, and black of all shades from the lightness of her own skin to the deepest ebony. The language that flowed around her also amazed her. People from strange lands, speaking strange tongues, mingled with those speaking English. And wonder of wonders, the man driving the carriage told her she would soon be boarding a ship to take her farther into the North, farther away from the dangers of slave hunters. Mathilde could see the blue of the sea in the distance. She'd never seen it before, having spent her life in the Virginia hills.

The closer they came to the ocean, the stranger the sights became. A one-legged sailor hopping along on a crutch. Women wearing paint on their faces, dressed as no decent woman ever would. A fist fight in front of a pub. A dirty-faced boy who reached into the pocket of a well-dressed man, relieving him of his wallet. The bronzed face and long black hair of a native. The ebb and flow of all life seemed to swirl around her the closer they came to the docks.

The carriage came to a stop, and the driver helped Mathilde alight. He carried her carpet bag, containing an extra dress and shift and the comb gifted to her by a Quaker lady. He firmly cleared a path through the throng for her, leading her to the gangplank of a ship. The driver took her by the arm and stepped onto the gangplank of the ship Matinicus. She stumbled a bit, surprised by the movement of the boards beneath her feet. He steadied her and helped her onto the ship. When he let go of her arm, she lurched against the railing as the ship bobbed about on the water. With a grin, the driver said, "Steady on, you'll get used to it." He tipped his hat to her and said, "God be with you," then he descended the gangplank and disappeared into the crowd.

Mathilde stood on the deck, at a loss as to what she was to do. Alone for the first time since the Stultzes had set her feet on the path of the underground, Mathilde stood on the crowded deck. Never before had she stood alone like this. She had no master to tell her what to do. No kind soul to direct her. She was on her own. The awesome responsibility of that aloneness flooded her. She alone was responsible for what she did next. At first, the thought terrified her. But as she stood on the open deck, breathing the salt air, feeling the sea breeze through her hair, she felt the stirrings of a force so powerful, it took her breath away. "This is what freedom means," she whispered. "Making my own way with no one saying what I should do but me. This is freedom." She raised her chin and pulled back her shoulders, standing proud for the first time ever in her life. "I am free. I am free."

Mathilde

Portland, Maine

June 1851

Nell Fessenden put the finishing touches to her work in the guest bedroom. The room once belonged to her brother Pitt when they were children. Now it was a resting place for visiting family or friends. Sometimes, too, for others who were on their way from one place to another. She gave the pillows one last fluffing and smoothed the wrinkles from the coverlet. Looking around the sunny room, she nodded her approval. The room was ready for the guest they were expecting that day.

Heading down to her father's study, she knocked respectfully at the door, "Father, all is ready upstairs."

Her father looked up from the letter he was writing to Pitt in Washington, D.C. "Good, my dear, I believe our guest arrives about 2 o'clock on the Matinicus. Will you join me at the dock to welcome her?"

"Of course, Father," she replied. Then she added, "Why is it, Father, that you write so often to the boys, but never to me?"

"Oh, haven't I written to you before?" asked General Fessenden.

"No, sir," she said teasingly, "When you are away, you send letters to mother and the boys, but never to your only daughter. Have I no need for your fatherly council?"

Samuel Fessenden replied saying, "Perhaps one of these days I will surprise you."

Nell said, "I shall wait for that great day with eager delight." She turned and walked out of his study, leaving her father with an affectionate grin on his face.

At the appointed hour, the General called to his daughter and with her hand on his arm, they walked the short distance from their home on India Street to the docks on Portland's busy Commercial Street. Scanning the docks, the general said, "Ah, there she is. The Matinicus. A fine looking ship. Let's see what interesting packages have arrived." Walking to the end of the gangplank, he and Nell ran their eyes over the faces of the passengers.

Seeing only one dark-skinned face, Nell waved her arm wildly to attract the attention of the woman in question. As she walked down the gangplank uncertainly, Mathilde looked toward Nell with consternation. Who was this cheerful young woman? Standing next to her was a handsome square-jawed man with twinkling blue eyes. Nell met Mathilde at the end of the gangplank. "I believe we are here to meet you. My name is Nell and this is my father, General Fessenden."

"Pleased to meet you," Mathilde replied shyly.

Nell rattled on, "We've fixed up Pitt's old room for you to stay while you're with us. The whole family is anxious to meet you. All except Pitt. He's in Washington right now. You'll have to tell me everything about your trip and all the places you've been." Nell's kind chatter soon put Mathilde at ease. General Fessenden took her bag to carry and at first she resisted, not used to a white man carrying her burdens. But he insisted with the firmness and manners of a military man, and she relented.

As they walked back toward India Street, Mathilde tried to soak in as much of her surroundings as she could. Portland was not as large a city as Boston surely, but still there was much going on around her. Arriving at the pleasant entrance of the India Street house, the party stepped into the front entryway, closing out the noise of the city. Taking Mathilde by the elbow, Nell showed her upstairs to the room she would occupy while she was in Portland, however long that might be. Mathilde looked around the sunny bedroom with a question on her face. She was used to sleeping in attics or barns, not a fine room like this. Nell, seeing her uncertainty, laughed saying, "Father insists that should any fugitives come to our house they will find not just a room where they may hide but a whole house where they are welcomed guests." After seeing to her comfort, Nell left Mathilde to settle in, telling her to join the family whenever she felt ready. They would dine at 7:00.

After Nell left, Mathilde stood looking around her. She peered through the windows into the street below and saw the every day life of the city passing along below her. Yawning, she looked at the big, comfortable bed with its colorful bedspread and thick pillows. Then, going to the side of the bed away from the door, she lay down on the braided rug next to the bed and fell asleep.

Mathilde was awakened later by a soft knock on the door. She jumped up from the floor, looking for a hiding place. The knock came again and a soft voice called, "Mathilde? It's Mrs. Fessenden. Time for dinner, dear." Feeling shy and awkward, Mathilde slowly opened the door. Mrs. Fessenden looked at her kindly. "I'm so sorry I wasn't here to welcome you when you arrived. My son Pitt's wife Ellen is feeling poorly, and I took some soup up for her." Mrs. Fessenden chatted away about family matters as the two women walked down the stairs. She told Mathilde about her sons and her grandchildren and neighborhood happenings, hoping to ease Mathilde's nerves.

They entered the dining room, and General Fessenden rose from his chair to pull out first his wife's chair and then Mathilde's. Shyly, she sat down looking at the dishes, the silver, and the linens on the table. Surely she was not meant to sit at the table with them amidst all this finery. General Fessenden smiled at the faces around the table, then bowing his head, he began to pray. With a blessing sought, the food was passed around amidst laughter and news of the day. As Mathilde sat with the family, it occurred to her that they treated her as an esteemed guest, rather than a despised runaway. Relaxing a bit, she helped herself to mashed potatoes and gravy, enjoying handling the delicate china with the gold rim. She sipped wine from a crystal goblet. She wiped her mouth carefully with the snowy white linen napkin as she'd seen others do.

When dinner was done, the family went into the parlor, and Nell played songs on the pianoforte, singing in a sweet voice while her father joined in with a fine baritone. As the hour grew late, Mrs. Fessenden said to Mathilde, "My dear, you must be exhausted from your trip. It's time we all retire." Leading the way up the stairs, Mrs. Fessenden entered the room Mathilde was staying in. Going to the bed, she chattered companionably while she turned down the bed and fluffed up the pillows. She said to Mathilde,

"My dear, you simply must try out this feather tick. I think you'll find it far more comfortable than the rug."

Mathilde dipped her head and her cheeks flushed. Mrs. Fessenden pretended not to see. She continued on, "Why, Mr. Frederick Douglass slept in that very bed, and he swore it was the most comfortable bed he ever slept in." The name caught Mathilde's attention. She'd heard of Frederick Douglass from the family she'd stayed with in Boston. The Fessendens welcomed a black man into their home and let him sleep in this fine bed?

Mathilde spoke softly, "I thank you, Missus. You all been so good to me."

Mrs. Fessenden smiled, placing her hand on Mathilde's arm. "Think nothing of it, dear. You are our guest for as long as you like. And please, you must call me Deborah."

Mathilde lifted her eyes up and gazed into the kind eyes of this woman who opened her home so willingly to a stranger and saw again that same light she had seen in the eyes of women who had helped her all along the way. Those brave, comforting souls who reached out to another woman in distress and with healing in their hands, raised her up from her knees.

On Saturday afternoon, after Mathilde had been in Portland for two days, General Fessenden accompanied Mrs. Fessenden and Mathilde on a social call. Taking the carriage, they traveled the short distance to Munjoy Hill. Alighting from the carriage in front of a large building, General Fessenden swung open the gate and entered the door without knocking. Mrs. Fessenden followed with her hand on Mathilde's elbow urging her forward. A man was standing at the front of the room focused on the book he held in his hand. Glancing up at the sound of the door opening, a wide grin came across his brown face. Striding down the aisle, he shook the general's hand enthusiastically and gave a small bow to Mrs. Fessenden and Mathilde. "Welcome! What brings you here this day?"

General Fessenden nodded to Mathilde as he addressed her saying, "May I present the Reverend Freeman of the Abyssinian Meeting House? Reverend, this is our new arrival from the South, Mathilde."

Beaming, the minister shook Mathilde's hand, saying, "Welcome, Sister! Please, let's all sit down." He ushered them onto benches.

General Fessenden lowered his voice and said, "Mathilde arrived on the Matinicus two days ago. We'd hoped to send her by ship to Nova Scotia. Unfortunately, I'm told the docks are being watched very closely by our enemies. We need to find a safer passage for her. I thought we might send her to Bridgton to my relatives. They can see her safe through to Lovell and then on to my sister-in-law's family in Canaan, then over into Canada."

At the word Canaan, Mathilde's eyes grew large. Reverend Freeman glanced at her with a question in his eyes. Mathilde spoke up quietly, "Mama used to sing to me about Canaan Land. I thought it was a pretend place."

"No, my dear," said the general, "I assure you, Canaan is a real town. My sister-in-law was born there." Mathilde sat in wonderment. To hear that name after all those miles of singing as she put one foot in front of the other. To hear she might really go there, she felt her apprehension slip away. She was bound for Canaan just like her Mama told her. On her way to Canaan Land.

Mathilde

Sebago, Maine

June 1851

Mathilde lay rigid on the dirt floor of the cellar hole, locked in vivid nightmare. Young Massa's face in hers and the stink of sweat and whiskey on him. His hands tearing at her clothing. The scraping of a barrel across the floor woke Mathilde with a start. Brushing back the fear of the nightmare, she tensed as the trap door was opened and a sliver of light entered in. A white man's face looked down at her. The same white man who helped unload the wagon the day before. "Are you well?" he asked. She nodded dumbly. "My wife fixed you a breakfast plate," he told her, handing it down to her.

She carefully took the plate in her hands and looked at it with wonder. This was no crude slave's plate. It was the plate a lady might own with a delicate feel to it and flowers around the rim. She'd seen such plates in Massa's kitchen where her mother washed them after each meal. And she'd seen plates like this in every white lady's house along the way. She looked questioningly at the white man. "Eat up," he said. "Got to keep up your strength. Another leg of your journey happens soon enough." She fell upon the food and ate ravenously.

After breakfast, Mathilde dozed fitfully, not knowing when she would be taken from the cellar and always fearing discovery. She was awakened hours later by the same white man. He was holding a lantern and motioned for her to climb up out of the cellar. "Stay quiet," he whispered, "The tavern is busy this noon." He led her to a farm wagon and helped her in, pointing to a false compartment covered with sacks of grain. When she was settled, he loaded more sacks to conceal her hiding place. Mathilde covered herself with an empty grain sack as best she could and huddled in a ball waiting for whatever would happen next.

While she lay waiting, her mind wandered back to her life on the plantation. With an ache in her heart, she thought of her mother stirring up a thin soup to feed to the field hands at noon time. Mathilde was assigned to help her mother almost as soon as she could walk. She learned to fetch soup fixings and polish silver. She learned to put together a pretty breakfast tray for the Missus to have in her bedroom. She fed chickens and collected eggs. And most importantly, she learned to be a well-behaved slave, to say "Yes, Massa," and "Yes, Missus." And to be always biddable. Mama told her that would keep her safe from punishment. Mathilde knew all about punishment.

When another slave was punished, the overseer called all the slaves together to watch. She'd seen her first whipping when she was still tied to her mother's apron strings. She was too young to understand why the slave man was whipped, but she remembered the sound of the whip and the screams of pain. To avoid a similar fate, she set out to be the perfect slave.

She succeeded in escaping punishment until her thin frame gave way to the first blush of womanliness. It was then that young Massa had started be-deviling her. At first, he would tease her or slap her. That soon gave way to groping when he thought no one could see. She tried to make sure she was never alone. Always wary, looking over her shoulder and around corners. Then came the day he caught her coming back from gathering mint from the herb garden. Grabbing her by the hair, he dragged her screaming behind the drying shed.

Mathilde shuddered in her hiding place in the wagon. Best not to remember that now. Who knew what horrors still lay ahead of her this night. She heard men's voices and made herself as small and still as she could. She felt the creak and sway of the wagon as one of the men swung himself up into the seat. She heard him say, "HUP!" and the wagon began to roll.

Mathilde

Doctor Jonathan Fessenden's House

South Bridgton, Maine

June 1851

A pounding at the kitchen door brought Mrs. Fessenden running. A frantic knock at the good doctor's door could only mean one of the neighbors was in trouble. She opened the door and saw one of the Ingalls boys, hat in hand and panting hard. He gasped out, "Mam's took bad. Pa says Doc's gotta come right off!" Doc Fessenden had heard the frantic knocking and was already heading for the door with his black bag in his hand. At 59, the country doctor was well used to springing into action at a moment's notice. He had brought many of his neighbors into the world and seen too many leave it.

Giving his wife a quick peck on the cheek, he whispered to her, "There's a wagon coming at dusk." She nodded in acknowledgement and gave the Ingalls boy a dipper of water while the doctor hitched his horse to the carriage. As the wagon left the crossroad and headed down Ingalls Road, she turned her hand to preparing dinner for her family, cutting off a larger than usual slice of ham and making a double batch of biscuits.

With dinner underway, Mrs. Fessenden began pulling the firewood from the wood box built into the wall to the left of the fireplace. Stacking it on the floor, she revealed the small entryway leading to the hidden room behind the chimney. Hearing the sound of a wagon, she glanced out the window, expecting to see the farm wagon Dr. Fessenden had spoken of. Instead, she was startled to see the carriage of Esquire Nat Littlefield pulling up in the dooryard. Calming her nerves and smoothing her hair, she hurried to the front door to intercept him lest he decide to come to the kitchen door instead. She opened the front door and greeted him with a touch of frost in her voice, "Squire Littlefield, what brings you by this evening. I trust your family is all well, and it's not a doctor's care you're seeking."

"No, no, Missus," he replied, "Just taking a drive about the neighborhood and thought I'd drop in to pay my regards to your good husband."

Fighting back the urge to glance up the hill to see if the expected wagon was coming, Mrs. Fessenden replied, "Alas, my husband has been called away to help Mrs. Ingalls in her time of travail."

Squire Littlefield stood on the porch looking suspiciously about. "Perhaps I should wait for him," he suggested.

Mrs. Fessenden replied with a calm she could only pretend, "He has only just left. I do not expect to see him for hours. He will be sorry to have missed you, Sir." She glanced over her shoulder toward the kitchen, saying "I'm so sorry, I must run, or my biscuits are sure to burn." Shutting the door in the face of the sputtering lawyer, Mrs. Fessenden leaned against the door frame to calm herself. Littlefield peered about the grounds, looking toward the barn and sheds before climbing indignantly into his carriage and continuing on down Fosterville Road toward the church nearby.

Mrs. Fessenden returned to her kitchen and quickly put the firewood back into the wood box to keep the hiding place from being discovered in the event that Littlefield returned. An hour later, Mrs. Fessenden again heard the sound of a wagon. Glancing out the window she saw the expected wagon coming down over the hill. Taking off her apron, she carefully hung it on its hook.

Opening the kitchen door, she stepped out to the dooryard, waving to the driver. Coming close to the wagon, she said quietly to the driver, "Littlefield left not long ago. I fear he is suspicious and will be coming back. I dare not let you leave your delivery."

"Yes, Ma'am," replied the driver. "How 'bout I leave a few bags of grain here as a decoy, and I'll take the rest of the load to the next stop."

Mrs. Fessenden nodded in agreement. She stepped away from the wagon and called out, "You can unload those bags right into the barn." Saying a fast and fervent prayer, she went back inside the house.

After unloading a few bags of grain, the wagon driver turned the wagon around and headed on down the hill until he arrived at the home of the local pastor, Joseph Fessenden, Dr. Fessenden's cousin. Pulling into the dooryard, he saw the pretty face of a young woman peer out the window. She came to the kitchen door and stepped out on the porch. "Well, Mr. Frost, what brings you here on this fine evening?" she asked.

"Well, Miss Phebe," he replied, "I come over to see my best girl, that's all."

"Why, Mr. Frost," she said with a twinkle, "What will your wife ever think of that?"

"Well, Miss Phebe, she knows you ever were my best girl. Don't suppose it will come as any kind of surprise to her. Now, step lively, girl, and tell your good Aunt I have a special delivery for her. Gotta get this grain unloaded so's I can git on home for my dinner."

Phebe glanced at the wagon bed and back at her neighbor. He nodded his head. Phebe said, "I'll let Aunt know, and I'll fetch

Uncle to open the barn door for that grain."

When the wagon was safely in the barn, Leander Frost swung down from the wagon seat. "Well, Parson," he said, "There was a bit of difficulty making this grain delivery at Doc's house. Littlefield is prowling around again."

"Let's get it unloaded and see what we've got here," said Parson Joe Fessenden. "I know the Missus is anxious to start her ministrations." The two unloaded the grain sacks, exposing the false compartment. A scared, black face looked out, taking in the two white men. Parson Joe reached out a hand to her. She looked into his blue eyes and saw only kindness. She slowly reached for his hand, wondering if touching a white man's hand would get her in trouble. He nodded and motioned, "Come, now, girl. You're safe here. My good wife is waiting for you with a good bowl of stew. I hear tell she's made me a fine blueberry pie for dessert. I wouldn't mind sharing a slice with you."

Leander spoke up saying, "Well, Parson, if your wife has made a blueberry pie, I might have to stay to supper so's I can have a slice. Your wife makes the best pie in the village. Just don't tell Apphia I said so."

Mathilde took the parson's hand, and he helped her climb down from the wagon. Just then, Mrs. Fessenden came out into the barn. "Oh, my dear," she said, coming toward Mathilde, "Welcome, to our home. Come right inside so we can make you comfortable after your journey." Taking Mathilde by the hand, Mrs. Fessenden led the girl into the house. Stepping into the big kitchen, Mathilde was greeted by the heavenly smells of chicken stew and fresh blueberry pie. Her stomach growled, and she looked down at the floor, embarrassed.

Just then, Mrs. Fessenden's niece came into the kitchen with a couple of dresses over her arm. "Aunt, I didn't know what size she was so I brought one of my dresses and one of yours." Stopping still, young Phebe looked Mathilde up and down. Mathilde hung her head in shame. She was filthy from her travels. She knew her hair was matted and unkempt. She could smell her own body odors. She stood there in the tidy, clean kitchen nearby the white women who were so neat and clean, and she nearly wept with the shame.

Young Phebe glanced at Aunt. Aunt said, "Oh, dear, where are my manners. What is your name?"

Mathilde continued to look down at her feet, cracked and dirty, and murmured, "Mathilde, Missus."

"What a lovely name! Is it French?" asked Phebe.

"Don't know, Young Missus," she replied, "Just the name they gived me."

"Well, Mathilde, it's lovely," replied Mrs. Fessenden. "Now, Phebe cut off a big piece of Mrs. Fitch's cheese to tide Mathilde over until we have dinner. Then, take her to the pantry sink and let her wash up a bit. I think your dress will fit her just nicely. She's no bigger than a minute, just like you."

Phebe led Mathilde to the pantry, chattering away to help Mathilde feel less awkward. She showed Mathilde where the soap was, fetched her a cloth to wash with and left her to clean up saying, "You take your time, and when you're ready, you come right back to the kitchen."

Mathilde slowly took off the plain dress given to her by the Quaker family who sheltered her in Pennsylvania. In all its plainness, it was the best dress she had ever owned. It was torn and stained from her journey from Quakertown through the woods into

New Jersey, but she couldn't think about that now. She pumped water into the basin the girl had left for her and began to wash away filth from her face and hands. As she cleaned herself, she looked around the pantry. It was neat and tidy like the white women. The shelves were carefully arranged with jars of canned goods—jams, pickles, string beans, row after shining row. To Mathilde, who had fed on only minimal food on the plantation, and that only the coarsest of meal and the produce not fit for Massa's table, the pantry with its variety of food, the delicious smells of spices, and the colorful array seemed to indicate this family was well to do.

She dressed in the girl's dress with its lace and buttons and cheerful calico print and just for a moment let herself feel like she was a clean, white lady in a neat, comfortable home. Then, she shook off her reverie, knowing that slave women could never live such a life. She opened the pantry door and shyly stepped into the kitchen.

"Oh, my dear, Mathilde," exclaimed Mrs. Fessenden, "You look lovely in that dress. The blue of the flowers sets your eyes off just right." The reminder of the shame of her birth brought a blush to Mathilde's face. Mrs. Fessenden pretended not to see, turning to the wood cookstove to stir the bubbling pot of stew. "Now, we'll eat as soon as Uncle comes in from milking the cow."

Young Phebe began setting the table, laying out four places. Mathilde said, "Oh, Young Missus, allow me do that! I did it back there for Missus. I know how." Phebe handed her the stack of plates, and Mathilde laid them out, looking at the flower pattern on each. "Sho' is pretty dishes, Missus."

Just then, Parson Joe came in from the barn carrying a milk pail which he carefully took into the pantry. Coming back into the kitchen, he dropped a kiss on his wife's cheek, saying, "Well, now, my dears, what have you put together for a feast tonight? I know I smell some of your good cornbread. What else do we have?" Mathilde thought he seemed quite a kind man.

The three white folks sat down at the table while Mathilde hung back. Mrs. Fessenden looked over and said, "Don't be shy, dear, sit right down." Mathilde had been treated the same way when she stayed with the Quakers and the Portland folk. Asked to sit down with the white people to break bread. She dipped her head and slid into the proffered chair.

Each family member reached out their hands to each other and to Mathilde. They bowed their heads, and Parson Joe began to pray, "Gracious Father, We thank you for the food you have provided for us and the hands that have made it. And we thank you for delivering our sister, Mathilde, safely to our home. We ask you to bless her on her travels and to bring her safely to the end of her journey, wherever that may be. In Jesus' name. Amen."

As Mrs. Fessenden ladled stew into bowls and Phebe passed around the cornbread, Mathilde sat looking around in wonder. These strangers had brought her into their home, given her clothes to wear, a place to stay safe, and good food to eat. The Quaker families had all done the same. These families seemed to think it was a natural occurrence to welcome a filthy, escaped slave into their homes. This family chatted together about the affairs of the village, explaining to Mathilde who each neighbor was, recounting funny stories of Leander Frost, the blacksmith who had driven the wagon that delivered her. In the warm glow of the kitchen and the good company of the parson's family, Mathilde began to believe that she just might be able to find a safe place in the world where she could live.

The sound of a passing carriage shook Mathilde from her thoughts. She looked up fearfully as the carriage slowed and came to a stop. "Quickly, get her into the pantry," urged Parson Joe. "I'll go to the door." Leaving the kitchen, he headed into the hallway leading to the front door. Glancing out of the sidelights on the door, he saw Nat Littlefield climbing down from his carriage. He glanced around the dooryard and walked to the front door. Parson Joe opened the door and said, "Well, Squire, what brings you to our part of town?"

Littlefield glared at him with contempt. "Don't play the innocent with me, Parson. I know you and your slave-loving family are up to something. Word is you're hiding slaves, and I mean to find out where. You know the law. Anyone helping a slave escape is guilty of a crime. I will not stand by while you break the law of the land. And you being a parson, you ought to be upholding that law."

Parson Joe gave Littlefield a stern gaze. "Good Sir, let us be clear on one item. I will support no manmade law that causes me to go against the laws of God. So, if a Child of God shows up on my doorstep from any walk of life or circumstance, you can believe with all certainty that I will follow the dictates of my conscience and will do for the least of my brethren as Christ would have me do."

"Ah, save your sermonizing for Sunday," spat out Littlefield, "Just know your actions are being carefully watched. If I so much as catch sight of a black face in these parts, I will bring down the law on you." Turning on his heel, he returned to his carriage and drove back toward town.

Parson Joe carefully closed and locked his front door and returned to the kitchen. "All is well, my dears," he said, "Now, let's talk about that blueberry pie."

After the kitchen was tidied up, the family gathered around the fireplace in the front parlor with the curtains drawn against the night and any peering eyes. Mrs. Fessenden pulled out the latest letter from Will Barrows. She read his most interesting account of a trial he was working on in his law practice. He sent many kind wishes for Aunt, Uncle, "Little Phebe," and Mary. Then, Phebe shared her latest letter from Mary who was away teaching school. Mary talked of how trying her pupils could be, but she seemed content and well. She spoke of coming home as soon as the school year ended.

Mathilde sat looking around the cozy parlor, listening to the chatter of everyday life, so far different from the horrors she had seen in her young life. This family was so kind and welcoming. She found herself wishing she could stay on, but she knew the danger was too great to even consider that to be a possibility.

As the evening waned, Mrs. Fessenden looked to her husband and softly asked, "Where do you think we should have Mathilde sleep tonight? Where will she be safest?"

Parson Joe replied, "I had thought to deliver her back to Jonathan's for safekeeping, but with Nat prowling the neighborhood, I think it best she shelter here. I think it's safest if she is close by. I don't want her in the barn alone. The safest place is likely the attic."

Mrs. Fessenden nodded and said, "I'll make up a comfortable spot for her." She stood up and turned to Mathilde, "Come, dear girl, let's find a cozy spot for you to rest." Taking Mathilde by the hand, she led her up the front stairs. Stopping in her own room, she opened a chest and took out a handmade quilt. She picked up a lantern from Mary's room, lighting it and handing it to Mathilde. She led Mathilde to a door at the end of the hall. Opening the door, she walked up a set of narrow wooden stairs to an open attic room. Even here, the house was neat and tidy. The room was set up with a few bedsteads. Mrs. Fessenden explained that they often took in student boarders who Mr. Fessenden taught. At the time, none were in residence. Mrs. Fessenden took Mathilde to the cot nearest the chimney. "You'll sleep warm and safe here tonight. Now, if there is anything you need, please let me know." With that, she went back down the stairs, closing the door behind her.

Alone again, Mathilde shone the lantern about the small chamber. She carefully unbuttoned the calico frock and folded it neatly at the foot of the bed. In just her dirty shift, she wrapped herself in the quilt Mrs. Fessenden had handed her and lay down upon the bed. Blowing out the lantern, Mathilde wrapped herself more tightly into the quilt. It smelled of cedar and sunshine. Closing her eyes, knowing that for now she was out of harm's way, she soon fell into a deep sleep.

***

In the deep stillness of the night, Parson Joe and Mrs. Fessenden were awoken by terrified shrieking. Parson Joe leapt from bed, reaching the door in one stride and flinging it open. He saw Phebe's white face peering from her chamber door. "It's Mathilde," she said.

Parson Joe yanked open the attic door and rushed upstairs, his night shirt flying. Mrs. Fessenden was fast behind him. "Phebe, get a lamp!" he shouted. Phebe came running with the lantern from her room. In the lantern's glow, they could see Mathilde huddled in a corner of the attic, sobbing. "My girl, what's wrong?" exclaimed the parson. He strode closer to her. She did not answer, only sobbing more as he got nearer.

Mrs. Fessenden moved closer and knelt down. "Was it a dream?" she asked. Mathilde nodded, still sobbing. Mrs. Fessenden looked to her husband and niece and said, "Let me have some time alone with her." They lit Mathilde's lantern and went back down the stairs leaving the two women alone.

Mrs. Fessenden took Mathilde by the hand and led her to her cot. She sat down next to her, putting a motherly arm around Mathilde's shaking shoulders. Mrs. Fessenden spoke soothingly. When Mathilde's sobs had subsided, Mrs. Fessenden gently said, "Now, come and tell me what your dream was about."

Mathilde shook her head, "I can't, Missus, it too ugly to tell you. You a good white woman, a God woman. You shouldn't hear such a thing." She began to cry again.

Mrs. Fessenden said, "My dear, you may find I know more of the harshness of life than you think. When I was about the same age as you are my dear father was murdered in cold blood. My family suffered terribly because of it, especially my dear mother. For years, I had nightmares about that. Please, do not think of me as any different from you. I am not. We are both women, and so we are sisters in the eyes of God. And sisters tell each other their secrets, just like my Phebe and Mary tell each other their secrets. Won't you tell me about your dream?"

Mathilde began haltingly to speak of the attack that sent her running headlong into the woods adjoining the plantation. As she relaxed in the presence of a wise and kind confidante, she began to tell the rest of her tale.

"After I run away, I was scared. I couldn't go back, and I didn't know where to go. I just run as hard as I could for as long as I could. I didn't have no food or blanket with me. Not no shoes neither. Just my dress that Young Massa tore. It didn't even cover me no more. I run through prickle bushes and got all scratched up. I knowed I should cross a river so's the hounds couldn't follow my scent. I followed the river downstream 'til I find a place I could swum across. I find a ole Injun path on the other side, and I followed that. It was getting dark, but I dasen't stop. I know Massa would be coming for me.

The fores' was dark, and I heared all sorts of horrible sounds, big crashes and coyotes howlin'. I liked to a-died from fright. I jes tried to stay on that Injun path. The moon give me enough light so's I could keep goin'. When the sun come up, I foun' a cave and crawl in. I was powerful hungry, but I dasen't go outside in daylight. They was leaves in the cave, and I went to lay my head down in 'em. A rattler near enough bit me. I jump back an' foun' a big rock, and I kill it. Couldn't light no fire to cook it. Jus' hadda scrape off the skin with a rock, and I et it. Made me sick I was in sich a state."

Mathilde buried her face in her hands as her shoulders shook from the memory. Mrs. Fessenden wrapped the quilt tightly around her and held her until the shaking stopped. "Tell me the rest of it, dear. It will do you a world of good."

Mathilde haltingly began again. "Soon's the sun went down, I lit outta that cave and walked all night. Then, I found a thicket and hid out all day. When night come again, I walked and walked. I seed a farm. I was powerful hungry, Ma'am, and I knewed it was wrong, but I went up to the chicken coop and stole an egg. It was jes one egg, Missus. Jes' one egg." She nervously glanced at the white woman.

Mrs. Fessenden nodded, "I would have done no different in your circumstances," she said.

Mathilde continued, "Dog set up a racket and the farmer came running with his shotgun. He shouted at me, and I took off running. That dog chase me and grab me by the dress and pull me down. Man came and shone a lantern in my face. I knew I goin' to die right then. Or worse, get sent back to Massa. But that man hollered 'Rebecca!' and this woman come out the house. She helped me up and wrapped her shawl round my tore up dress. She took me inside and set me at her table, and she fed me. Then she give me one of her own dresses to wear, and she give me a quilt to wrap up in. She give me food to take with me. Then, her man took me in his wagon and drove until we got to another farm. He told me I be safe there for the day."

Mathilde's jaw stretched into a yawn. Mrs. Fessenden asked, "Would you like to sleep again, dear?" Mathilde nodded her head, lying down on her cot. Mrs. Fessenden reached down and stroked Mathilde's hair back saying, "If you need me, I'm just downstairs. Sleep well, little one." Quietly she went down the stairs, leaving Mathilde alone again.

Mathilde lay quietly on her pillow with silent tears rolling from her eyes. Beneath this roof, she had known tenderness and care the likes of which she had never experienced. For the first time in her life, she felt accepted, safe, and valued. It was a feeling she knew she would never forget. When her tears were emptied out, she fell asleep and rested peacefully through the night.

Before sunrise, Mathilde rose and found her way to the kitchen. Looking about the pantry, she found the fixings for pancakes and a rasher of bacon. She busied herself in the kitchen starting coffee, mixing batter, and frying bacon. The family woke and came to the kitchen looking surprised. "Why, Mathilde," said Phebe, "You've made us breakfast! What a kindness you've done!"

Mrs. Fessenden rubbed a hand across Mathilde's shoulders saying, "Yes, thank you, dear! What a pleasure to have breakfast already made this morning." Parson Fessenden grabbed a piece of bacon from the serving plate as Mrs. Fessenden shooed him away with a kitchen towel.

Mathilde shyly served the food she prepared saying, "Jes' wanted to say I 'preciate the trouble you gone to for me, is all."

Parson Joe replied, "Our Lord Christ says when we help those who need it most, we are helping him. You are welcome in our home, Ma'am. And if these pancakes taste as good as they smell, then it is I who is most grateful. Now let us thank the One who provides for us all."

Freedom's Light
Portland, Maine

April 11, 1851

Free Coloured Man Sent into Slavery Under Armed Guard Numbering 300!

Boston citizen Thomas Sims arrested for being an alleged escaped slave. Abolitionists and lawyers fought to prevent his forced exodus. Taken by an armed guard of three hundred police and citizens.

The effects of the dastardly Fugitive Slave Act were once again felt in the seat of American liberty. Thomas Sims was arrested and jailed on false charges brought by his supposed master. Fearing reprisals from local abolitionists as in the case of Shadrach Minkins, Sims was taken to the docks under heavy guard and dispatched south while scores of brave men fought for his freedom in the courts.

It is reported that free men and women of color are making an exodus from American soil into Canada to escape the heavy hand of this government-imposed mandate. Freedom has again been dealt a heavy blow.

To Mr. Henry Clark, from Phebe Beach Fessenden

South Bridgton

July 12, 1851

My dear friend,

I received your letter when sick of a violent cholera attack occasioned by taking strawberries and cream with my supper. I am yet feeble, but will begin my answer, as it will not be safe on account of my health and a weak eye, to write much at one time, and I may be some days finishing it.

First then, to the passage I wrote on the paper I sent you. It was plain to see from your second letter to us in the remarks there made upon slavery, the fugitive slave law, the return of the poor young man, Thomas Sims, to slavery despite the efforts of abolitionists, the duty of ministers to keep the subject of slavery from the pulpit, and the passages of scripture offered, that your sympathies were against the slave. That you approved the system and the general provisions of the fugitive law.

Among the papers you sent us soon after this letter was half a sheet with no individual article on it but the one signed Sigma and short advertisements. The author of this article attempted to prove that the Old Testament sanctions slavery—that it was an institution allowed by God to the Jewish church for the preservation and prosperity of which he gave laws and regulations. As this was the only article in the paper which could possibly interest us and as some of the closing passages were the same in spirit and similar in expression to parts of your letter, we had every reason to suppose you intended that article for our special attention.

Yourself and Sigma both lamented the existence of slavery. Four pages of your last letter were directly or indirectly devoted to the subject of slavery. At the conclusion of your letter you say, "Ask Mrs. Fessenden if I am not orthodox and if there is anything in this letter she cannot say amen to." With my mind upon the views of slavery expressed in your letter and the article aforementioned and my eye upon the injustices and evils of this system, a notice of which I read in the Freedom's Light and with a conviction this having been appealed to for my assent to your views, I ought to deal plainly.

I wrote the passage you transcribed. Is it disrespectful in me to ask a friend why he does not practice upon his principles? If a gentleman is contending for the use of alcohol as a beverage and, in support of his opinions, he refers to the laws that have protected the making and selling it and to the good and respectful men who have truly used and manufactured it. The scriptures which countenance it, "give wine to those that be of heavy hearts, let him drink and forget his poverty and remember his misery no more." "Take a little wine for the stomach's sake." And the example of the Saviour himself who turned water to wine for a wedding entertainment, would it be unkind or impolite in me to ask him, if it is right to use alcohol as a beverage and the Bible sanctions it, why not engage in the making and vending of the spirits yourself? If this gentleman professes to lament the evil consequences of the traffic of spirits to individuals and society, the question would seem to be no more impolite.

Or if an East Indian missionary should from the same authorities defend polygamy—tell me of the many wives of the patriarchs and David and Solomon. Godly men, and this the Bible says expressly, that "God gave David his views" and still should defend the evil results of this custom in its mischievous influence and the impossibility of introducing the pure principles of the gospel when it prevails, would it be disrespectful in me to ask the defender of what we consider adultery if it is right? Why trouble yourself about results? Why not take to yourself a dozen wives and get on smoothly with your neighbours? I do assure you, Dear Sir, I had no unkind feelings in my heart toward you, nor did I intend the least disrespect.

In your last letter, you tell me to "reflect on what I wrote and realize what it implies and whom it implicates." I have reflected on what I wrote and think I realize what it implies; to my own mind it implies these things. It implies that binding and selling slaves is an important part of the business of American slavery. This everyone knows in many of the states it would be a bankrupt concern altogether but for the internal slave trade. It implies, too, that if you and Sigma prove from the Old and New Testament that God approves its component parts, it implies also that after you have proved that God sanctions slavery, it is somewhat like being wise above what is written to lament it as "an evil." Again, it implies that all that God approves is right and honourable, and what is right and honourable for one man is right and honourable for another. That if it is right for a Southern planter to bind slaves for the market, it is right for Lucius M. Sargeant, it is right for Deacon Henry Clark. I think it was Newton who said, "If God should send two angels to this world, the one to rule an empire and the other to sweep up the streets of a city, they would have no choice as to the office they should perform."

As to whom what I wrote implicates, it implicates no person, but principles. From the manner in which the questions were put in the Freedom's Light, it must be obvious to everyone that I supposed the thought only of engaging yourself in the cruelty and debauchery which is part and parcel of slavery would be absolutely shocking to you. You will see now that the veritable intention and meaning of that question was to show to yourself the verdict of your heart and conscience upon this subject, and how rejoiced I am, my dear and long-cherished friend, to find that your heart and conscience are with us. Your letter to me abundantly shows that you consider yourself insulted at the bare mention of a vague possibility of coming in personal contact with your principles—principles which your intellect defends from the Bible.

Again you say in your last letter, "Examine what I did write, reflect on it seriously and then let me have your mind frankly." I have examined and reflected upon the subject of your letter and will endeavour to give you my mind frankly and respectfully. This I am the more willing to do. In case it may be that I have not heretofore been frank enough and so have given you reason to think I had no mind or feeling upon this subject, I have ever believed that my husband, from his intimate acquaintance with these subjects was a more suitable and able defender of them than myself and have not feel called upon to say so much as I should have done in other circumstances. After your introduction and a few remarks to Mr. Fessenden on political parties, etc. you speak of the constitutionality of slavery and the right to reclaim fugitives. I will begin here.

When God tells me he has "made of one blood all nations," I believe he means to include the African nations. That the African is a man, entitled, as much as any man, to "life, liberty and the pursuit of happiness." I look upon him as my neighbour whom I am to love as myself; as my brother whom if I do not love him, I can make no pretensions of love for God, whom I have not seen. Of course I think it is wrong for any man or body of man, by any power that can get up by parchments or armies or what not, to make a slave of an African as it would be to make a slave of me.

I think it as great a breach of the gospel law of love and Christian courtesy to send the coloured man to the "nigger pew" in the church, the forecastle of the steamboat, and the "Jim Crow" of the rail car, as to thrust me into these degrading situations. It seems to me that it is as cruelly wrong to treat a coloured man with such injustice, scorn, and neglect as destroys his self-respect and happiness here and compels him to abandon his native country for a foreign and strange land as it would be to treat me thus. And all are as much bound to seek the education and elevation, every way civil and religious, of the poor coloured man, here at his proper home (here though he may be by human enactments) as they are to seek the good of poor white men.

God says to me, "If there be among you a poor man, in the land which the Lord thy God giveth thee, thou shalt not harden thine heart nor shut thine hand from thy poor brother, thou shalt open thine hand wide unto thy brother, to thy poor and to thy needy in thy land. To my mind, this does not look like the sort of "poor pappy" sympathy or pity, a kind of commingling of contemptuous pity, which holds one at arm's length and then says, "God help you." This kindness is to be shown to "thy brother" "in thy land."

When I see a fugitive from slavery and look upon him as one whose rights have all been cruelly wrested from him—whose sensibilities and affections have all been wantonly outraged and who at every cost and the endurance of every hardship has escaped from a degrading bondage which not God but avaricious oppressors and wily politicians have thrust him into. And so that he has fallen among thieves who have stripped him of all, even his manhood—the scars of the slave—whip, chain, and iron collar are ample evidence of their murderous intentions, shall I pass by on the other side, or should I obey the Saviour—pity, comfort, and relieve him? God says to me "Thou shalt not deliver unto his master the servant which is escaped from his master unto thee—he should dwell with thee, even among you, in that place which he should choose in one of thy gates. When it liketh him best, thou shalt not oppress him." Shall I obey God, or shall I shut my gate upon him and thrust him back to slavery? "Whether it is right to listen unto men more than unto God. Judge ye."

I consider these the hungry, thirsty, naked, imprisoned, and afflicted ones, yes the very little or insignificant ones, my feeling for whom and conduct toward whom will be the test of my acceptance with the Saviour in the great day. "In as much as you have not performed these acts of kindness to these despised ones, ye have not done it unto me." You say of this "Fugitive Slave Law" there is no new principle introduced in it, some of its details are not well and should be altered, but there is "no reason for all this stir about a few fugitives." O, my dear sir, you cannot view this subject as I do, or you would never speak this coldly upon it. It seems plain to me that the moral relations of slavery are sustained by the legal ones, as the branches are nourished and sustained by the root! And to these moral relations you never can have given your attention.

I feel that what ever others may think of the social relations between free women and slave women, yet before God, they belong to the same sisterhood. That they are my sisters, and when I know that a million and a half of my own sex are held in chattel slavery, at the mercy of unprincipled men—not a wife among them all— who have never been taught that they have a higher or holier purpose than to suckle slaves and be the victims of the uncurbed passions of slaveholders—whose life is a various and vagrant concubinage, traversing the circle of overseer, master, master's sons, and master's guests—who have no power to defend their own chastity, or of resisting the lustful tyrants by whom they are surrounded—on whose behalf no husband, father, brother, friend, or lover dare raise his arm to defend them from brutal outrage— and that the young and handsome, whose beauty of form and face attract the gloating eye of passion are ripened for the New Orleans markets where in Southern harems they are obliged to lead lives of indescribable loathsomeness.

When I know these things, should I not be a patroness of licentiousness—a defender of the huge Southern brothel, if I did not, with all the zeal and power God has given me, speak out in condemnation of them, ill will or "bad spirit" though I be charged with? Yet should I keep silence, or speak softly on this subject, even you sir, and every other virtuous man must suspect me of impurity or condemn my timidity. However others might regard me, I should despise myself.

But to return. Suppose that one of these unfortunate beauties should have got from some accidental source an idea of what constitutes a virtuous and noble woman and the shame and sin of the life before her and that in the works of another she finds herself on the way to New Orleans—suppose by almost super human power and adroitness, she should escape and should tread her solitary and darksome path for hundreds of miles toward the north star—should lie down in caverns with poisonous reptiles by day and pursue her lonely journey by night, finding the wastes of the forests less to be dreaded than man; should swim rivers and keep off famine by roots and insects, until at last, thanks be to God, she sets her mangled and bleeding feet upon the soil of freedom.

Perhaps some echo of the Pilgrim mothers has reached her ears. She has heard of Boston and its noble women of old, and she hies thither as to a city of refuge—as to a sanctuary where virtue has an altar and where she can lay down her hunted and weary body and be at rest. Fallacious hope! The lecher pursues his prey; he is there. He goes to some lawyer who serves out a warrant. He goes to some constable who serves it. The victim is seized at midnight under some lying charge, and she is carried before some commissioner. Here, a process is gone through which she does not understand, and some papers are read of which she never heard and then a judgment is pronounced that her labour is due to her pursuer (and such labour!). That she owes service to him (and such service!), and then the commissioner delivers her into his arms.

Now, how ought I to regard such a law? A law that instead of encouraging the aspirations for light and liberty and rewarding the heroic efforts of my sister—instead of inciting her to goodness and protecting her in virtue, turns her over to the body's shame and the soul's perdition! A law which, if she comes to my door and appeals to me for help, forbids me to feed or clothe or shelter her! A law which threatens me with pains and penalties severe for this forlorn fellow being the very same kind offices which Jesus Christ commands me to do at the peril of my eternal salvation! As a woman and a Christian, ought I not to spurn it? And as I would incur the approbation of my final Judge, ought I not to glory in every opportunity of trampling it under my feet?

And how ought I to feel toward the northern Senator, that traitor Daniel Webster, without whose influence this odious bill would never have become a law? This man, whom, heretofore, we have all delighted to honour who was born and educated in the land of the puritans who has long sat under the banner of New England's praises and received the emblems of the Saviour's sacrifice at New England altars? I cannot but feel this—that the statesmanship and moral bearings of this measure indicate strongly that what is said of him is true; viz. that his intellect has become influenced and bewildered by strong drink, and his sense of virtue has become deadened by gross sensuality. Ought I to feel any respect for such a man? In view of his dissolute character and his untold injuries his influence has procured for my sex, can I be true to the sacred interest of virtue myself and not regard him with detestation?

In speaking of the propriety of bringing political and other exciting subjects into the pulpit, you say that you consider that on the Sabbath ministers should preach the gospel only. I agree with you, my dear sir. That all unnecessary labour and parade, even to bury the dead is inconsistent with the right observance of the Sabbath. I do not believe, as I presume you do not, that the Mosaic Law on the Sabbath ought now to be enforced. The penalty of which was death for the slightest violation. Of course, I try to understand the instructions of the New Testament upon this subject. I see that for no cause did the Pharisees so carefully watch and so passionately censure the Saviour as for his violations of the Sabbath.

The church and parish here are perfectly united in Mr. Fessenden, and his salary is punctually paid. Our meetings, we are told, are better attended, according to the population, than any in the vicinity. Mr. F. is called upon more frequently than any minister in the conference to lecture in towns about us, and his lectures are not confined to slavery. A year ago when the minister at the center of this town was dismissed, Mr. F. was applied to take his place; the village has become large and is rapidly increasing. The people assured Mr. F. if he would consent to remove they should be better united in him and could raise a better salary for him, than any other man. I don't say these things boastingly, nor from any estimation Mr. F. is held where he is best known. That is the opinion of competent judges well-acquainted with his public and private ministrations, his mind has not become so engrossed with the evils of slavery, as to interfere with his usefulness, nor that "it is thrown off its balance, so that he cannot rightly divine the word of truth."

I presume husband will not thank me for what I have said, for he feels that he has ever given half the sympathy and effort to the injured slave which he will wish he had done, when he meets him at the bar of God. Perhaps I ought to make some apologies before I close—one, for what many might call "indelicate allusions," but I confess to have none of the mock delicacy which is more offended at the sound of guilt than its substance; and to believe that one can even begin to appreciate the horrors of slavery while ignorant of or indifferent to its polluted and polluting character. And too, my letter is very long, but I could not say frankly what I thought and felt upon these subjects without talking a good while.

Ever your devoted friend,

Phebe B. Fessenden

Mathilde

South Bridgton

July 1851

A knock sounded at the front door, and Joe Fessenden looked up from the sermon he was writing. His wife ushered in Dr. Pease. "Well, Doc, what brings you all the way from town?" asked the parson.

"Bad news, I'm afraid," he replied. "Nat Littlefield is making it tough to get a delivery through. We'd planned to take the package up Lewiston way and then east to New Brunswick, but Nat's got spies watching the roads. The package can't remain here. It's too hot and rumors are flying that a man from down South has been in Portland asking questions about a package he's missing."

Parson Joe nodded his head, thoughtfully. "I thought that might be the case. I think I have a plan. My wife's sister lives in Canaan, Vermont, right on the border. If we send the package that direction, we could get it into Canada pretty easily if we send it care of my sister-in-law. She's delivered a couple of packages in the past. My wife's family owns property on the other side of the border, so it's not unusual for them to go back and forth."

Dr. Pease nodded his head. "I think we've got to put that plan to work. The package needs to leave quickly."

Joe nodded, "Understood. I will have my wife send a letter to her sister to expect delivery. I'll make the arrangements on this end." Dr. Pease shook Parson Joe's hand and bid him good day.

Mathilde

Road to Canaan

Early August 1851

Leander Frost had always been an early riser. His sister Mehitable insisted he distrusted the rooster to get his job done. In truth, he liked to rise up and get a jump on the day. Plus rising before his wife gave him the only peace he was likely to have from the constant clacking of her tongue. His Apphia had a good heart, but Land! How she could run on. Today, he had a bit of a journey ahead of him. He needed to make a delivery and get back in time to take care of the business of the day. Someone's horse was always in need of shoeing, or a farmer's plow was sure to break. He'd been thinking about taking on an apprentice to help him, but the right one hadn't come along yet. His nephew Arthur showed some promise, but he wasn't quite old enough yet. Hitching his horse to the small wagon, he sprang up into the seat and drove next door to the Fessenden's house.

The parson heard his wagon coming, and he quietly stepped out of the shadows with a second shadow following him. Making no sound, he helped a shadowy figure into the back of the wagon, covering the form with rough burlap sacks. He gently patted an arm and said a silent prayer. Stepping back from the wagon, he melted back into the pre-dawn darkness. The wagon slowly rolled down the dirt road, making as little noise as possible. Traveling by the still pond, the horse began the slow incline up the back side of Choate's Hill and down the steep grade that required such firm control of the wagon.

As dawn broke over South Bridgton, Reverend Fessenden came to the breakfast table looking tired. Mrs. Fessenden stood behind his chair resting her small hands on his shoulders. He placed his hand on hers and said nonchalantly, "Well, dear friend, what shall we have for breakfast this morning. Perhaps a slice of that leftover mince pie?"

Leander Frost rolled his wagon into Abraham Barker's homestead at daybreak. Jumping down, he tapped on the front door. Barker opened the door and seeing Leander at such an early hour, he asked no questions, going directly to the back of his wagon. Pulling away the burlap with great gentleness that belied his title of Strongest Man in Lovell, he looked into the exhausted face of Mathilde. She looked back at him with a mixture of fear and curiosity. "Come on out, Sister," he said boldly. "You have nothing to fear here." He helped her out of the wagon and led her to the front door. Turning to Leander, he said, "You look like you could use a cup of coffee." Leander grinned and said, "I wouldn't turn one down." The three entered the front door, and Mrs. Barker turned from the fire with the coffee pot already in hand. Smiling, she put two more cups on the table.

Abraham Barker helped Mathilde into the saddle. She was unused to riding, but she was tired of bumping around in the backs of wagons. A few hours in the fresh air on horseback would be a welcome change. Mr. Barker had said he was taking her as far as the White Mountains, and she'd go by stage through the mountains. Mrs. Barker had given her a light wool coat, stitched by the ladies' sewing circle at her church. They'd added a sturdy petticoat and long stockings. Mathilde was unused to the early morning chill in the air, part and parcel of the vagaries of Maine weather. She shivered in the saddle with every breeze. Plodding along the winding dirt roads of Western Maine soon gave Mathilde a sense that the jouncing of a wagon might have been preferred to the soreness of riding to one who is unaccustomed to the activity. She hung onto the saddle, a picture of misery, and a steady rain began to fall.

They traveled on for mile after mile, Mathilde desperately hoping their destination was just around every bend, only to be disappointed to see still more forest and another bend in the seemingly unending road. At last, Mr. Barker turned to her saying, "We'll arrive in just a few more minutes." Mathilde nearly cried with relief. Plodding into town, Mathilde saw muddy streets and small buildings. Most of the residents of the town had left the streets to the dismal rain, drawing inside near fires and cookstoves that burned off the damp. Pulling his horse up at the livery stable, Barker swung easily down from his horse. He stepped over to Mathilde's horse, and, reaching up, he swung her easily to the ground and held her for the fraction of a second she needed to get her feet back under her after a day on horseback.

He led the horses under cover, and Mathilde waited for him while he and a groom rubbed the horses down and gave them hot mash. Then, going next door to the town's only hotel, he asked for a room, paying the bill. She looked at him questioningly. He handed her the key saying, "I'll be heading back home as soon as I've had a fast meal. The hotel keeper will put you on the stage tomorrow. You're nearly there," he said encouragingly. With that, he took his leave, wishing her safe travels.

The next morning, Mathilde climbed up to the front seat of the stage coach next to the driver. Even here in this land that was so close to freedom, she was still not allowed to ride in the comfort of the inside of the stage. But the sun was rising high, and the sky was the blue of sea in the morning, and she felt her spirits rise. Under her breath, she hummed, "I'm on my way, on my way to Canaan Land, Had a mighty hard time, but I'm on my way, on my way to Canaan Land."

Mathilde

Canaan, Vermont

1851

Abigail Beach Perkins tucked her sister's letter into her apron pocket. She stood looking out of the kitchen window remembering her childhood and how Phebe had been as a second mother to her, especially after their dear father was murdered. Her thoughts flowed on to the difficulties she'd caused her sister and brother-in-law when she'd stayed with them in Kennebunkport and South Bridgton. Oh, she had been a foolish thing. She knew that now. She had gotten caught up in the follies of youth as much as her brother Samuel had done. She'd caused Joe and Phebe some serious embarrassment by her actions. Having a rebellious young sister underfoot at the parsonage had been a trial for them both. In the end, their uncompromising principles and unconditional love had set Abby on a better path. Now, caring for her mother in Canaan, Abby was anxious to repair whatever damage she had caused by her foolish actions. Phebe had asked an especial favor of her, and she was prepared to grant that favor to the best of her ability.

Two days later, a pair of weary horses pulled the stage coach down Canaan's main street, carrying an exhausted passenger. They came to a stop at the Beach's house. The driver swung down and reached up, helping a woman alight. Swaying with exhaustion, the woman stood a moment until she got her balance. Going to the kitchen door, the man knocked. Abby Perkins opened the door with a look that mingled curiosity and excitement. Looking into the face of the woman who stood wearily on the doorstep, she held out her hands saying, "You must be Mathilde. Welcome to Canaan."

South Bridgton, Maine

September 1852

Phebe entered Joe's study quietly. Poor man had been under such strains of late. She'd fixed him a good lunch to cheer him up. She expected to find him hard at work preparing his sermon for the following Sunday. Instead, she saw him slumped down on his desk, his head bowed down on his arms. Alarmed, she quickly went to him, touching his arm. "Joe! Are you ill?"

He looked up, startled. "I'm sorry, my dear, I did not hear you enter." Phebe looked into his red-rimmed eyes and realized he had been weeping. Her Joe, weeping. He was such a strong man, such a rock for everyone else during trying times. Seldom had she seen him like this. Undone, weary, discouraged.

"Why, Joe, what is it! What is wrong?" He shook his head, saying nothing. "You're frightening me, Joe! Please tell me."

Joe looked at her tiredly. "Phebe, I just don't know if anything I've done in my whole life has mattered one bit to anyone. I feel like a failure. Like I have let Holy God down. What is the point of writing one more sermon against slavery? What have I done that has made one bit of difference? I have fought the good fight. Tried to help others as Christ would have me do. And what have I gained by it? I've been threatened with tar and feathers, hung in effigy, persecuted by my neighbors, put my family through all of that, and to what purpose? Men are still intemperate, ruining their lives and hurting their families. Slavery still holds its grip on this land. I feel as though my life's work has been for naught. When I stand before the judgment seat, I will have little enough to show for my years on earth."

Phebe looked at Joe with tenderness in her eyes. This dear man who had meant so much to so many. Had helped so many neighbors and strangers. Could he not see what he had done? In the parlor, Joe heard his niece Phebe, his beloved adopted daughter, playing a tune on the piano and singing in her sweet alto voice. Looking at his wife, he said, "At least there is that to show. Our girl grown up to be a fine person, a bright light in the world."

Phebe replied, "Yes, Joe, think what might have happened to her if you hadn't fought for her as you did. And she is by far not the only life you touched. Your parishioners love you. Your neighbors know they can always count on you when times grow difficult. Your family, my family all know how much you have helped them. And Joe, you have ever taken a stand against what is wrong. Always been a champion of what is good in the world. You have stood strong for those who needed a voice and for those whose chains bound them to a life of degradation. Can you not see that? I surely can."

Joe listened to all she said. In his heart, he knew there were many he'd helped along the path. But there was still so much work to be done. God's work seemed never to end. Heartened by his wife's words, he gave her hand a squeeze saying, "I think I know how to finish my sermon now. I thank you." Picking up his pen he wrote, *"Grow not weary in this fight. It must be forever so, that in this land of the free, strong committed men and women will take a stand to root out and destroy every impediment to equality. Let not ignorance, nor fear, nor tradition, cause any soul to live in chains beneath freedom's wing."*

Mathilde

Coaticook, Quebec

September 1852

Mathilde stood looking at the front of a small run-down cabin. Scraggly weeds surrounded the steps, and vines ran unchecked all along the edges of the house, threatening to pull it down. The only sign of the cabin having once been a home was the small stunted rose bush in the dry dust by the front door. On it was one small bud, all the bush could produce under so little care. In her hand, Mathilde held a carpet bag. The carpet bag held her best dress made of green checked gingham, the gift of the ladies of the local church, a new shift, and a well worn quilt, a gift from the Quaker family who owned the cabin. Wrapped within the quilt was her one precious possession. She pushed open the cabin door, a little crooked on its hinges, brushing away the cobwebs. Looking in, she saw a crude bedstead with a straw tick and a rickety table. The rest of the tiny space was bare.

Mathilde quietly walked in and sat her bag on the table. She turned in a circle, taking in the room. The cabin's one window was covered with fly specks and grime. The ticking on the bed showed signs of mouse activity. In one corner was the small skeleton of some animal. As she inspected the room, Mathilde heaved a sigh. Walking to the door, her door, she slowly closed it. Leaning against it, she felt the sturdiness of the wood at her back. This was her door. A door she could close or open at her will. A door she could use to shut out the world or to fling it wide to welcome a friend. She need not fear a master who intruded at night bent on forcing his will upon her. She need not fear the slave stealer in this land where slavery was banned. This door. This simple wooden door that most folks took so much for granted, gave her power over her own self, over her world. She could open the door and walk out across the field un-accosted. She could return home at the end of the work day and open that door and be welcomed. Close the door and be safe inside. Once inside, she could order her day, her household, as she saw fit. To have a door...this is what it meant to be free. To have a door. A door of her own.

Crossing to the table, Mathilde opened her carpet bag. She pulled out her extra clothing, shook each item out carefully to remove the wrinkles. She hung them neatly on the wall pegs. She gently pulled out the quilt, carefully laying it on the table. Reaching within the folds of the quilt, she pulled out an item, setting it with great care upon the table. Taking the quilt to the bed, she brushed off the mouse droppings from the ticking and draped the quilt over the mattress, admiring the workmanship. The Quaker woman called it a log cabin quilt. The colors were vibrant and brightened the dingy room. At the center of each block was a red square that symbolized the hearth. The quilter had sewn light-colored strips on one side of the hearth square and dark colors on the other side. The light and the dark, day and night, sunshine and shadow. Mathilde smoothed the cover, arranging it to her liking.

Then, turning to the table again, she picked up her one precious thing. Holding it in her hands, she traced the delicate flowers with her calloused finger. It was a real China plate. The kind of plate a lady would have, given to her by Mrs. Perkins. The plate was covered with tiny pink roses, delicate and sweet. It had a small chip on the back but that didn't matter to her. She had a plate like a lady would have. A real lady. A lady who had respect. A lady who had a home. A lady who had a door. She carefully placed the plate in the center of the table. She stood back and looked around the cabin. The pink roses on the white plate, the green of the gingham, the bright calicos of the quilt all brought sparks of color, warming the room.

She thought of all the kindness of the people she'd met on her way from her old life. People who had endangered themselves and their families to help her—a stranger, a fugitive, a slave. Where once there were shadows, now there was sunshine. The dark and the light just as her quilt portrayed. At the center of it all was the hearth of the heart. Hers and so many others who had lifted her up along the way. Mathilde sat on the edge of the bed and watched the sunbeams coming through her window and the sun shining brightly on her rose plate. Then, rising, she set about the simple homely tasks of tidying the house. "This is being free," she thought. "A door, a plate, a quilt, and a floor of my own to sweep. Praise God!"

Separating Fact From Fiction

Soon after the completion of *Wild Sweeps the Wind*, I received an other worldly visit. This is not an unusual occurrence by any means. This visitor was quite insistent that I get the details right. She introduced herself to me as Mathilde. I asked, for clarity's sake, "Is it Mathilde or Mathilda?" She was quite firm with me on this point. She was Mathilde. I sat down and wrote the opening passage of this book where she begins to tell her story.

Honestly, I did not know who she was or why she was talking to me. I had no plans for such a character in the book I had not started to write yet. But, strange occurrences are the norm for writers, so I took it for what it was…whatever it meant. Over the first months of writing this book, Mathilde stopped by quite often, telling me a little more about herself each time.

A few months after her first "appearance" in my life, I was working on my research at the Bridgton Historical Society and I came across quite an interesting letter. It seemed to have been written by Joe Fessenden. It was his writing, on his usual sermon-writing paper. As I read through it I was quite impressed by his ability to shape an argument. Then I came to a line where the writer mentioned that she usually left such things up to her husband. Backing up, I realized that this letter was written not by Parson Joe, but by his wife. It was she who was so masterful at shaping an argument. As I read through the second time, I was so very impressed that a woman of her time was so scholarly, so educated, and so well-written.

As the letter continued, Mrs. Fessenden began describing the plight of the women who were held in slavery. She said of female slaves:

That they are my sisters, and when I know that a million and a half of my own sex are held in chattel slavery, at the mercy of unprincipled men—not a wife among them all—who have never been taught that they have a higher or holier purpose than to suckle slaves and be the victims of the uncurbed passions of slaveholders—whose life is a various and vagrant concubinage, traversing the circle of overseer, master, master's sons, and master's guests—who have no power to defend their own chastity, or of resisting the lustful tyrants by whom they are surrounded—on whose behalf no husband, father, brother, friend, or lover dare raise his arm to defend them from brutal outrage—and that the young and handsome, whose beauty of form and face attract the gloating eye of passion are ripened for the New Orleans markets where in Southern harems they are obliged to lead lives of indescribable loathsomeness.

Suppose that one of these unfortunate beauties should have got from some accidental source an idea of what constitutes a virtuous and noble woman and the shame and sin of the life before her and that in the works of another she finds herself on the way to New Orleans—suppose by almost super human power and adroitness, she should escape and should tread her solitary and darksome path for hundreds of miles toward the north star—should lie down in caverns with poisonous reptiles by day and pursue her lonely journey by night, finding the wastes of the forests less to be dreaded than man; should swim rivers and keep off famine by roots and insects, until at last, thanks be to God, she sets her mangled and bleeding feet upon the soil of freedom.

Perhaps some echo of the Pilgrim mothers has reached her ears. She has heard of Boston and its noble women of old, and she hies thither as to a city of refuge—as to a sanctuary where virtue has an altar and where she can lay down her hunted and weary body and be at rest. Fallacious hope! The lecher pursues his prey;

he is there. He goes to some lawyer who serves out a warrant. He goes to some constable who serves it. The victim is seized at midnight under some lying charge, and she is carried before some commissioner. Here, a process is gone through which she does not understand, and some papers are read of which she never heard and then a judgment is pronounced that her labour is due to her pursuer (and such labour!). That she owes service to him (and such service!), and then the commissioner delivers her into his arms.

This letter showed me why Mathilde had come to me with her story. Her life was the ribbon that would weave through the story, giving slavery the human face, the beating heart, the scarred soul that made it such a heartbreaking evil. Was she real? I do not know. But, how could Mrs. Fessenden have known with such detail, such feeling, the plight of the slave unless she had been exposed to these matters in a personal way.

The Underground Railroad through Bridgton is a documented fact. Samuel Fessenden's involvement was well-known. The houses in Sebago and Bridgton that are featured in the story are real and both have generations of oral history of their use. They each have a room that could well have served as hiding places for escaped slaves.

All other characters in the book are real, with the exception of Mathilde and the characters with whom she interacts before her arrival in Portland.

Joseph Palmer Fessenden was born October 24, 1792 in Fryeburg, Maine and died on February 13, 1861 in Bridgton, Maine. Phebe Beach Fessenden was born October 20, 1796 in Canaan, Vermont and died on February 21, 1870 in Bridgton, Maine.

Voices of Pondicherry

For more information about Bridgton, Maine and the Voices of Pondicherry series, visit:

www.VoicesofPondicherry.com

To contact the author:

Caroline Grimm

c/o Church Mouse Publishing

P.O. Box 605

Bridgton, Maine 04009

cdgrimm@VoicesofPondicherry.com

Bibliography

Beach, Phebe F. Journal. Schlesinger Library, Radcliffe Institute, Harvard
University.

Bordewich, Fergus M. Bound for Canaan: The Epic Story of the Underground
Railroad, America's First Civil Rights Movement. New York: Amistad,
2006. Print.

Fessenden Family Papers. Bridgton Historical Society, Bridgton, Maine.

Fitch, Edwin Peabody. Ninety Years of Living. [Portland, Ore.]: Evangeline
Fitch Moke, 1976. Print.

Gordon, William. Journal. Fryeburg Historical Society, Fryeburg, Maine.

Horwitz, Tony. Midnight Rising: John Brown and the Raid That Sparked the
Civil War. New York: Picador, 2011. Print.

Joseph Palmer and Phebe Beech Fessenden Papers, George J. Mitchell
Department of Special Collections & Archives, Bowdoin College
Library.

Lowance, Mason I. Against Slavery: An Abolitionist Reader. New York:
Penguin, 2000. Print.

McPherson, James M. Battle Cry of Freedom: The Civil War Era. Oxford:
Oxford UP, 2003. Print.

Price, H. H., and Gerald E. Talbot. Maine's Visible Black History: The First

    Chronicle of Its People. Gardiner, Me.: Tilbury House, 2006. Print.

Reed, Rebecca Perley. The Story of Our Forbears. Salem, MA: Higginson Book,

    [19-. Print.

Shorey, Eula M., and Cara Cook. Bridgton, Maine, 1768-1968. [Bridgton, Me.]:

    Bridgton Historical Society, 1968. Print.

Siebert, Wilbur Henry, and Albert Bushnell Hart. The Underground Railroad

    from Slavery to Freedom: A Comprehensive History. Mineola, NY:

    Dover Publications, 2006. Print.

ABOUT THE AUTHOR

Caroline Grimm moved to Bridgton, Maine with her family when she was seven years old. She grew up surrounded by historic houses, steeped in stories of the past, and her curiosity got the better of her. She immersed herself in local history for the sheer joy of uncovering the past lives of neighbors long gone. She wrote her first paper on the topic in high school. Since that time, she is often found haunting cemeteries, poring over fragile letters, reading crumbling newspapers, tramping across far flung battlefields, and traveling down forgotten roads. Her neighbors sum up her odd behavior by shaking their heads and saying, "She writes."

BY THE SAME AUTHOR

Voices of Pondicherry series:
Wild Sweeps the Wind, *Book One*

Cash Flow Wizard series:
Stop the Cash Flow Roller Coaster, I Want to Get Off...
What Every Small Business Owner Should Know About Cash Flow, But Most Don't
Strength in Numbers*:*
The Entrepreneur's Field Guide to Small Business Finances

With Co-author Perley N. Churchmouse:
Dear Church Folks*: Letters from Perley Churchmouse*
God's Own Mouse*: More Letters from Perley Churchmouse*
Church Mouse on a Mission*: Letters From Mouse Haven*

11069723R00129

Made in the USA
San Bernardino, CA
06 May 2014